CHAMBER OF HORRORS . . .

The little chamber, buried deep in the living rock of the old schloss, reeked of evil and pain. Rader and his men did not wear black hoods and masks, but the effect was the same. They were torturers—about to do a job.

The young baroness' feet were already anchored to the rack. She was fighting the hand manacles, screaming with terror.

Nick took a last look around him: Rader, the two at the rack, and the two near the door. They had machine guns . . .

The curse of the golden statue with the ruby eyes was about to claim another victim . . .

THE NICK CARTER/KILLMASTER SERIES

NICK CARTER

A Killmaster Spy Chiller

EYES OF THE TIGER

AWARD
BOOKS
NEW YORK

Dedicated to
The Men of the Secret Services
of the
United States of America

Titles are also available at discounts in quantity lots for industrial or sales-promotional use. For details write to Special Projects Division, Award Books, 235 East 45th Street New York, N.Y. 10017.

EYES OF THE TIGER

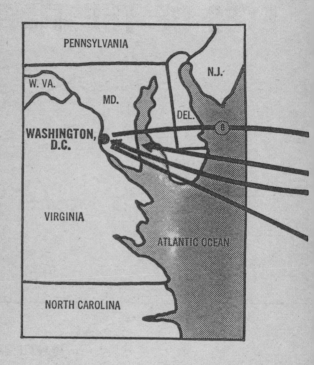

LEGEND
— Nick Carter's Route

PENNSYLVANIA

W. VA.

MD.

N.J.

DEL.

WASHINGTON, D.C.

VIRGINIA

ATLANTIC OCEAN

NORTH CAROLINA

N
W—E
S

SPAIN

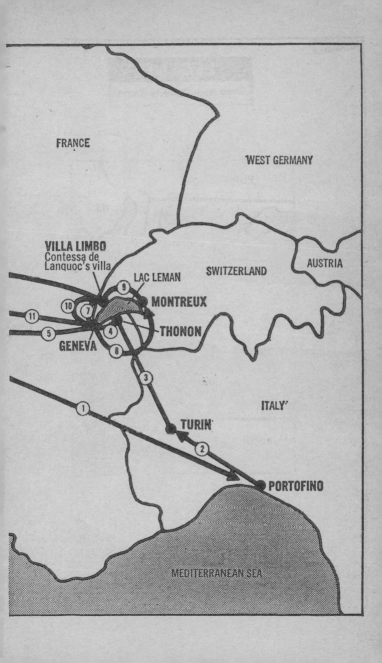

One

There had been the girl in Portofino last night—the girl who had given herself to me with passion and tenderness. She had been a dark-haired girl with a sylph's body and a beautiful smile, and she had shared the joys of the soft Italian night with me. She had also shared the wine and the stars and the music, and, finally, my bed. And I, who lived always on the edge of danger, walked always in the shadow of death, had taken the girl and been grateful and left her sleeping. Headed for Turin and Geneva. Mission Tiger was beginning!

Now there was another girl. She was sleeping, too, because I had just given her knockout drops. A Mickey Finn!

This girl was a knockout herself. Honey blonde, lovely and lithe, a Nordic type with a chiseled patrician nose over a full, sensuous mouth. Her lips were parted in silent invitation as she slumbered on the ragged sofa in my cheap hotel room in Geneva.

I had come into Switzerland early this morning, crossing on the last boat from Thonon in France. I had been dressed as a deckhand, had actually worked as a deckhand, and I would have sworn nobody could see through my cover. But it looked very much as though someone had—and if that was so, the fat was right in the fire. Mission Tiger was blown before it got off the ground! And I, Nick Carter, Agent N3, old man Hawk's number-one boy, and KILLMASTER for AXE, was losing my touch.

I frowned down at the sleeping girl. I *wasn't* losing my touch, of course. I *never* could. I'd be dead the minute I did. Without bragging or boasting, I knew damned well that I was close to perfect at my job, and he knew it. When you had worked for AXE as long as I had, and were still alive, you were as perfect in your job as any man could get. Simple as that.

I paced the dingy little room. I was still wearing the shabby, dirty working clothes. No one back at AXE in Washington would have recognized me, probably not even Hawk, but that could be changed in ten minutes. I glanced at the girl—she would probably sleep for another two hours or so—and kept pacing the little cage, my eyes moving constantly—scanning, probing, weighing, assessing.

There was nothing to fear in this room; I already knew that. No bugs, no time bombs, no way in which a listening device could be beamed into the room. It was just a cramped, dirty room in a cheap Geneva hotel. No one could have made any preparations—no one had known I was coming.

Or had they? It seemed impossible. Yet the girl was here!

Starting to feel a little edgy, I ran my hands through my hair, cropped especially short as part of the disguise for this job.

Job? Maybe there was no job. Not now. It *did* begin to look as though Mission Tiger had somehow been blown! I almost groaned. I had been looking forward to Mission Tiger as a nice change of pace. It was a simple matter of stealing the most expensive tiger in the world from the strongest bank in the world. The tiger stood a foot high, was eighteen inches long, and had the two biggest rubies in the world for eyes. It also happened to be made of solid gold. No use trying to put a money value on it—it was priceless. For a lot of reasons. A lot of people wanted the tiger—also for a lot of reasons.

And now the girl! Did she want it too?

I went to the sofa and stood looking down at her. Sleeping like a baby. A beautiful baby! Yet there was nothing particularly *young*-looking about her. I guessed her to be about thirty, give or take a year. Her face, in repose, showed faint lines that indicated experience, or even suffering. Her body, beneath a simple and expensive faille suit, was long and flowing. Good lines. Fine lines.

She twisted on the sofa, restless in her sleep, and her short skirt hiked up, giving me a delicious view of her long, slim, beautifully molded legs. Her knees were not quite together. An extremely provocative posture.

Gazing down at this pleasing vista, I made up my mind. It was but a small thing. I meant the girl no harm. Not yet, anyway. And I *had* felt something when we'd brushed together in the taxi on the way here.

I reached down and pulled up the girl's skirt.

It was not unpleasant work, if you could get it, and I certainly had it now. That was just it. It *was* work. My job!

It paid off. There were the two broad black garters around slim white thigh columns. Each garter supported a little holster. And in the holsters, nestling so innocently against their background of white satin, were a little knife and a little pistol.

Gently, I lifted the weapons from their sheaths, trying not to touch the sleeping girl's flesh—I liked my women awake. I pulled her skirt down again and took the weapons over to the room's single lamp.

It was not really a knife at all, but a small stiletto. A nasty little needle of Spanish make. It had blood grooves. The pistol was a "Lilliput," the smallest automatic made by Webley. I cradled it in the palm of my hand and grinned. Made a sound like a popgun, and would kill you just as dead as a Colt .45 if it got you in the right place. Or as dead as my own handgun, the terrible-tempered Wilhelmina, had made so many men who had thought themselves faster than me, and had been fools enough to put it to the test.

I walked over to the narrow, rump-sprung bed in one corner of the room. On it lay a massive Gladstone-type suitcase. It was made of rhinoceros hide and was covered with beat-up travel stickers. These stickers could be arranged in certain patterns to identify me and convey messages to other AXE agents. Gladstone, as I affectionately thought of the old bag, had been around. She was original issue. She had secret bottoms and sides, a score of little pouches and compartments containing vials and bottles and kits.

Old Mr. Poindexter, head of Special Effects and Editing at AXE, had built Gladstone personally for me. Little old Poindexter was something of a nut on gimmicks and gadgets, but he was the best in the world at his job.

I tucked the little gun and the stiletto away in Gladstone and was about to turn away, when I hesitated. I stared down at the bag. Had Gladstone been a mistake this time? Had it been *quite* the right luggage for a deck-hand on a steamer plying Lac Léman? Mistakes like that got you killed! Even the hangman can be hanged; even the executioner can be executed.

I shrugged and went back to work. Too late now. You never looked back anyway. Only forward. But someone had made a mistake! Somewhere. Somehow.

I inspected the sleeping girl again. Still out. Still long, lithe, and lovely, the beautiful Nordic face still showing faint lines of wear and worry. I pulled down her skirt again and went through her purse for the second time, just to make sure.

No better luck this time. The usual stuff: a compact, tissues, three lipsticks, a change purse, a half-empty pack of Players. French and German money, plenty of it, but no Swiss francs. Not surprising. She had crossed the lake with me—had in fact picked me up on the boat—and there had been no time to change money since.

Her passport was just as interesting, and puzzling, as it had been at first reading. West German. It described her as the Baroness von Stadt. Elizabeth von Stadt. Elizabeth? Surely that was an English name? I made a mental note to ask her about that in the future—if there was a future for either of us.

With the passport in hand I went to the sofa and studied the sleeping girl again. No doubt about it. This *was* the Baroness. At least it was her picture in the Baroness' passport.

She could be a baroness, I supposed. Her clothes were chic and expensive. There was even—despite the concealed armory—a hint of that ineffable sense of class and distinction one associated with such women. I had known—and bedded—a lot of them, and I considered myself something of an authority on the subject.

I stuffed the passport back into her purse and stared at the stained ceiling. This was a minor Gordian knot. It was, in fact, a sonofabitch! If she was genuine, really the Baroness von Stadt, why had she thrown herself at me like a common prostitute? Why seek me out on the windswept stern of the steamer *Genève* and make an obvious pass! At me, of all people!

Because I was, or was supposed to be, a sort of low type! I was Herr Rubli Kurz, a laborer and lake roustabout, born near Zurich. I drank too much. I had the papers to prove all this. I spoke all four languages of Switzerland—French, Italian, German, and enough Romansh to get by. And when I was doing my job as KILLMASTER and playing a part, I didn't play it at all. I *lived* it!

I took another look at the girl, wondering. There were women, high-born women, who picked up rough types and wallowed with them in filthy little hotels. They took no pleasure in men of their own class. After they had satisfied themselves they went back to their own world and forgot the whole thing.

No. That would be too coincidental, and I had a life-long distrust of coincidence. In any case, *after* she had insisted on coming to the Hotel Lux with me, she had begun to act a little scared. She certainly hadn't been in any hurry, *then,* to drag off her clothes! Or mine. I couldn't just let her go, of course, not until I knew all about her. Maybe she was even a target for KILL-MASTER. Maybe she was a counterspy. Maybe she was an independent, trying to make a buck from any side. Maybe she was anything! Maybe even a high-class bitch with a yen for a fast romp with a big, strong, dirty man! But I had to *know!*

So I got the bottle of good wine out of Gladstone, always keeping between the girl and the door, and poured us both a little drink. And spiked her glass with a shot of old Poindexter's very special sleep inducer!

Now I had her. But what in hell was I going to do with her?

It would be dawn soon. I had to get out of there fast and talk to Hawk at AXE and find out what was going on. Maybe Mission Tiger was blown. Or maybe the little lady was only an eccentric whore. I had to know.

I trusted the sleeping potion with which AXE had so generously provided me, but I never took any chances I could avoid. I got the special straps and gag out of Gladstone and in one minute flat had the Baroness just where I wanted her. She would keep until I got back. I took the rhino-hide bag into the tiny bathroom. In a couple of minutes, Herr Rubli Kurz was going down the greasy drain.

Mr. Frank Manning, of Cleveland, Ohio, U.S.A., came out of the bathroom and went to inspect the sleeping girl. The gag wouldn't choke her, and I had checked to make sure she was not a mouth breather. I pulled down her skirt again. Funny how that skirt kept riding up—I wondered if it could be an indication of character or profession. I hoped neither. Mr. Frank Manning, of Cleveland, was a kindly man. He wished the girl well.

Mr. Manning did. But then, Mr. Manning was getting on a bit, graying, and had a little rubber paunch that could be inflated to suit the occasion. Mr. Manning was, in fact, a little flabby.

Nick Carter was quite another matter.

Not yet lost in the flabbiness of Mr. Manning, I bent over the sleeping girl and kissed her lightly on the lips. I sincerely hoped he wouldn't have to kill this lovely thing.

Bitterly, audibly, I cursed myself.

How could I have been so damned careless? I had overlooked one of the best and most common of women's hiding places!

Mr. Frank Manning sighed and retired for a time. He was too much of a gentleman for this sort of thing.

Carter wasn't. I unbuttoned the girl's thin blouse, with its lace jabot, to release a swell of white breasts over a black half-bra that concealed nothing. I wasted no more than a glance on the soft-firm pears, the pink areoles, the red cherry tips. I plucked the silver locket by the chain and drew it slowly up from the well between her breasts.

It was large, about the size of a silver dollar. I flicked it open and studied the picture in it for a long time.

Even I, who had seen so much of death and destruction, of butchery and brutality, even I could not restrain a grimace of disgust.

Two

The face in the locket—if you could call such a leering, contorted thing a face—was that of an elderly German officer. His blouse was open at the throat. I could see threads where collar insignia had been ripped away.

The man's face, even in the last agonies of a horrible death, bore the indelible stamp of a Prussian of the old school. *Junkers!* This type had hated Hitler, and Hitler had returned the hatred.

In this case Hitler had won. I immediately recognized the picture for what it was: one of a series of still shots, released after the war, from the motion pictures of the execution of German officers involved in the July plot on Hitler's life.

This man had been hanged with wire instead of rope —the wire was buried in the swollen flesh—and instead of the conventional gallows, a meat hook had been used. The method was neat, simple, and horrible.

The executioner had twisted a loop of piano wire around the condemned man's neck, hooked it over a meat hook suspended from a bar, and kicked away the chair or box on which the man had stood. Even I was sickened at the thought of the ensuing agony. There was no hangman's mercy, no breaking of the neck; there was only the slow, hellish strangling, the soundless agony, the pitiful dance on air that you could never breathe again.

A most undignified death. Hitler had meant it to be that way.

But who was the hanging man? And what was his death photo doing in a silver locket between a pair of lovely breasts?

I put the locket back where I had found it and re-buttoned her blouse. I patted her cheek.

"You're some kid," I said, "whoever you are! A gun, a knife, and a picture of an atrocity for a necklace. Either you've got a damned good reason for all this—or you're a nut to end all nuts."

The girl stirred and moaned in her sleep. Her face was flushed and the honey-blonde hair strayed in curling tendrils over her forehead. I brushed it back. She turned on the sofa, and I looked down the enticing white canyon of her thighs. I pulled down her skirt.

"I'm going to keep you around for awhile," I whispered. "You interest me, Baroness. You really do." Time would tell what she was. Who she really was.

Time!

I took a last swift look around the seedy room. The lock on the door wasn't too bad. There was no window in the bathroom. The single window in the room, grimy and cracked, was also locked. Hermetically sealed, by the look of it.

I peered through a patina of filth at a rusty fire escape. It twisted down four flights to a back area. I saw the shadows of boxes, crates, and garbage cans, and I realized that dawn was sneaking in fast.

In chill, surrealistic light, with the beginning shadows falling and clotting before me, the cobbles ringing hollowly, I made my way along narrow streets. At an intersection, I saw two policemen coming my way. I ducked into a shop door and waited, but they turned off. I sighed in relief. I wanted no trouble with the Geneva police, and it might be a little hard to come up with a genuine excuse for Mr. Frank Manning, staid and respectable businessman, wandering around alone at this hour in a strange city.

I came to the Quai du Mont Blanc and found a taxi rank, as I had known I would. The puffy-eyed chauffeur was annoyed at being dragged from his nap. He opened his mouth to complain, then closed it. If this paunchy, graying American wanted to go to some insane address in the worst and toughest part of Geneva, then so be it. He shrugged his fat shoulders over the wheel of his ancient vehicle and took off.

"Allons!" I commanded. *"Vite!"*

"Merde!" said the driver, under his breath. He thought I couldn't hear him.

Twenty minutes later, I entered a small and admirably equipped *dépôt* deep in the cellar of a nondescript and decaying building. It is doubtful if anyone other than the concierge and the few people who actually used it knew of its existence. Certainly the Swiss Government, and the Geneva police, did not. Or gave no sign if they did. American gold, as supplied in vast quantities by the American taxpayer, can work miracles.

One of the minor miracles in the place was the small but immensely powerful radio transmitter that, on demand, hooked instantaneously into the AXE phone system in the States.

There were two men in the *dépôt* when I was admitted. I had spoken a word, made a sign, showed a card. The heavy door had been unbarred. Now I had to face Hawk. Verbally, at least. I felt a slight sense of relief that it *was* only verbal—I still had the queasy sensation of having somehow goofed.

If I had—well, even over the radiophone, Hawk had a rough way with agents who goofed. I could visualize him doing it. Hawk, ramrod stiff, lean, cold-eyed, chewing on a dead cigar as he took the hide off a man.

But, even to save my sin-encrusted soul, I could not imagine *how* I had fouled up! Everything had been routine until the Baroness had entered the picture. Had *insisted* on picking me up.

Even the little adventure in Portofino hadn't mattered. I had often indulged in these little side trips, these pleasant excursions into fun, femininity, frolic, and a little wine. They did no harm when time was not important, and on this job, on Mission Tiger, it hadn't been. Or so I'd been given to understand at the final briefing. I wasn't exactly supposed to loaf, but I didn't have to rush either. I had rather looked forward to this one, to having a little extra time for once. All work and no play makes even Nick Carter a dull boy.

Hawk's voice, cold and dry, came over the scrambler.

"Nice of you to check in with us, Nick."

I felt a rising spark of anger at the tone, then extinguished it. You just didn't get angry with the Hawk.

"Sorry," I said. "I'll explain later. Right now I think we're in trouble here." Quickly I explained about the girl.

Hawk seemed relieved, rather than surprised or alarmed.

"So she did make the contact, eh? Good. I was worried about that. I thought it might get messed up. We had to move in such a goddamned hurry. That's okay, then."

"Is it? Who is she, for Christ's sake?"

Hawk was beginning to sound annoyed. "What do you mean, who is she? Didn't she identify herself? I know we didn't have time to get her the proper credentials, not with everything breaking at once, but she was instructed to try to intercept you—before you got to Geneva if possible—and identify herself and tell you to call me immediately for confirmation on her. That's one reason I'm not exactly happy with you, Nick. I've been waiting for your call for twelve hours now. Did she just make contact with you?"

I decided to let it ride for the moment. Maybe the

scrambler was doing its job too well. Things weren't making much sense. If I kept my mouth shut, maybe I could pick up a clue.

"Yes, she just made contact with me. I'll tell you later. What's so hot?"

"Just this. Both Rader and Hondo are on the move. Both obviously heading for Geneva. Probably there now. You might not have to figure an angle for getting that gold tiger out of the bank, Nick. They, or one of them, might do it for you."

I thought back to the briefing I had so recently received. Max Rader and Shikoku Hondo were the two men who had been under surveillance for months, even years, while AXE, and half a dozen other agencies from as many countries, waited patiently for them to make a move in the direction of the golden tiger. Now they had.

"I was sort of hoping somebody else would get the tiger out of the bank," I said. "Then I'll just take it away from them. Much easier that way. I never was much good at robbing banks. Especially Swiss banks."

Hawk was talking. "It can't be coincidence, naturally. Hondo left Tokyo two days ago. Destination Geneva. Presumed reason for visit, to sell cameras."

"Hmmm—not a bad cover, ordinarily. But in this case, not so good."

"Yes." Hawk's voice warmed a bit. "I almost get the impression that our Japanese friend doesn't really care if he's spotted or not. And I don't like it. Shows too much confidence on his part. Those two seem pretty sure of themselves."

"I'll see about that," I said. "I say if they *can* get the tiger, let them. The minute they do, they'll start trying to kill each other. Who knows, maybe they'll succeed. If they do, I'll just pick up the tiger and come home."

Hawk's voice dried out. "Don't be so sure, my boy. And don't underestimate Max Rader. He's the brains in that little twosome."

"I never underestimate anyone."

"Good. Don't. Well, Max Rader is on the move, too. He left Hamburg yesterday. And that's where we're in real trouble. Or you are." Hawk chuckled.

I grinned. My boss was sometimes given to something very close to gallows humor.

"As I started to tell you," I said, "I think the whole mission is in trouble. I think we're blown! Meaning me, of course. And if I am, I'll just have to come out in the open and dogfight with them. And you know how funny the Swiss are about brawls on their scenery!"

For the first time Hawk sounded worried. And puzzled. "What makes you think we're blown?"

"The girl, damn it! You say she was supposed to contact me, that she had no proper credentials, but would tell me who she was and I could confirm. Swell! But she didn't! Not yet, anyway. She just picked me up on a boat. For obvious reasons. I didn't know who in hell she was, and she didn't say. She was too busy acting like a—"

To my amazement, Hawk was laughing. "Is that all? And just imagine Nick Carter being worried about *that!* I've heard everything now. Don't you see—that's *her* cover! She would have backed off fast enough if it had come down to the real thing. Still—" Hawk turned serious again, his more usual manner, "I *can't* understand why she played it that way. But she'll explain, no doubt."

"No doubt," I said. "But in the meantime, a few questions. I—"

Hawk cut me off. "Let *me* ask a few questions. The real reason we're in this jam stems from one thing—you didn't report in from Turin yesterday. I was waiting for that call. I meant to tell you about the girl, the Baroness, then."

My throat tightened. So it *had* been my goof, after all. I hadn't been able to find the Turin man. There was only one man there, and the setup kept changing, and if you couldn't establish contact with him, you were out of luck.

I told Hawk about not being able to find the man.

Hawk didn't seem angry, only burdened. These things always happened, and always at the wrong time. "Not really your fault," he said. "The poor fellow died suddenly. Heart attack. Things got balled up and he wasn't properly identified for hours. We couldn't get another man in there in time to meet you."

I kept silent. It *was* my fault. After the Portofino adventure, I had been trying to make up for lost time. I hadn't thought that it had particularly mattered. This was supposed to be an easy one, remember? Anyway, I had given up after the first try at finding the Turin man. Given up and pushed on for Geneva, out of touch with AXE for longer than the prescribed period. Damn! Always when you were careless!

"This girl," Hawk said, "is quite genuine. Not AXE, of course. West German intelligence. She's the Baroness von Stadt. *That's* genuine, too."

"I'm flattered," I said. "It isn't every day I get to work with a Baroness. But just for the sake of clarity—why do I need her? You know I don't like to work with women!"

Again there appeared a hint of a chuckle in Hawk's tones. "You need this one," he said. "Oh, how you need her! And you should enjoy working with her. I understand she's very beautiful."

I sensed that Hawk, for some reason of his own, was enjoying himself. There might even be a spark of fun in those icy old eyes, a faint grin around the steel-trap mouth. I got the feeling that my leg was being pulled. Hawk *did* know how I felt about working with women. So if I *had* to work with one, somehow really needed her, that would amuse the old man. So let it. We were both in a deadly occupation, with no recognition for service, no reward but the grave. If you could garner a laugh now and then, so much the better. Even old Iron Pants. But I still couldn't see how . . .

"You trust this Baroness?"

Immediately Hawk was his old sour self again. "Do I trust anyone? But within reason we do. West German intelligence gives her a good name. *They* use her. Anyway, she was the best we could do on such short notice. Of course, you're not to tell her any more than is absolutely necessary about this mission. She's assigned to you, to help you. And as I say, you really need her."

"Why?"

"Because Max Rader has had his face changed! Plastic surgery. That picture you've got of him isn't worth a damn now. And the Baroness, your new girl, is the *only* one who knows what he looks like now!"

"That's going to make it real cozy," I said. "I can't work without her! She'll be little Miss Tag-along."

"That's about the size of it. Watch your step, Nick. If Rader *is* after the tiger—and what else *would* he be after? —the only way he's going to be stopped is by shooting him. He must be in Geneva now. And, if your cover *is* broken, he'll know who you are. Or might know. You can't be sure. But he can be sure that you won't know him—or he could be if we didn't have the Baroness on our side."

"Just one more thing before I go back to work. How did this—the Baroness—make me out on the boat? And why didn't she identify herself properly?"

"The first I can answer," Hawk said. "I committed a slight breach of security myself. I had to. No Turin contact, remember. So I told Bonn a few of the routes you *might* use getting into Geneva. And I told them about Gladstone. I told the Baroness how she could pick you up by the stickers on your suitcase."

"It's on your head," I said. "Well, okay. But I still don't like working with women. Women are for *after* hours."

"Just remember that. The Baroness is an agent, a temporary agent working for AXE. Treat her kindly, boy. Treat her very kindly! She's your eyes for the time being, as far as Max Rader is concerned. Without her, you wouldn't know Max if he asked you for a match."

I was beginning to like this less and less. But the cookie crumbled and that was that.

"How come *she's* the only one who knows Max Rader's new face?"

"I'll let her explain that. Better get back now, Nick, and start being kind to her. I suppose you've gone to ground already. Want to let me know where, just in case?"

"Hotel Lux for right now. Probably not long. I'll be in touch."

"I've got it. Anything else?"

"This Baroness—is she, I mean is she a little crazy or something?"

"Not that I've heard, and we've got a pretty good file on her. Bonn has the real stuff, of course. Why?"

I told him about the picture of the hanged man. I was careful not to explain how I had gotten a look at it.

"That must be her father," Hawk said. "There's a story of sorts about that—a legend, whatever. Don't know how much truth there is in it. He was hanged—"

"I saw the picture."

"Yes. Well, the story is that Max Rader had something to do with it. The Baroness carries the picture around to remind her to kill Rader sometime. She hates him like sin, or so the story goes. You know how rumors float around in this business."

"All pretty coincidental, isn't it?"

"Not as much as it appears. She's been on Rader's trail for years, I hear. Waiting for him to slip. Maybe he has now. You see, Nick, you won't have an unwilling helper. She *hates* Rader. She's dying to finger him for you. If you're not careful, she might kill him herself, if it comes down to that. So take good care of her. What did you say you did with her? She's at the Hotel Lux with you?"

"She is indeed," I told him. "Sound asleep. Very sound asleep. I gave her a Mickey Finn."

Three

When I left the *dépôt* I emerged into a dazzling mid-September morning. The air was as sparkling and clear as a fine Swiss wine; the early sun cast golden bangles on the blue waters of the Rhône as I crossed a narrow cobbled bridge. I decided to walk back to the Hotel Lux. There was plenty of time. The girl should sleep for another hour yet. I needed to stretch my legs, which had become somewhat cramped in the character of Frank Manning. I also needed to exercise my brain a bit—this mission was beginning to assume the complexity of putting a jigsaw puzzle together twenty feet under water.

Beyond the little bridge I paused to adjust my gait to the paunch and personality of Mr. Manning, then glanced about to get my bearings. In the distance I could see the old League of Nations looming on the horizon. An imposing stone monument to dead hopes. I stood considering it as I lit a Gauloise. It stood to the northwest of the city, in the Ariana Park sector. I had to make a right at the next opportunity and double back. Half an hour should do it.

A fat, puffy-eyed shopkeeper, taking down his shutters, gave me a *"bonjour."* I returned the greeting, in the atrocious French of Mr. Frank Manning, and trudged on. I was conscious of the man's eyes staring after me. Well, it *was* a little early for an industrialist from Cleveland to be up and about. I increased my pace a bit, puffing as a man out of condition might, and kept to narrow

25

allées, away from the main streets, as best I could. My thoughts went back to that first briefing in Hawk's office three months earlier.

The briefing had been brief indeed! Hawk, with his usual saturnine glance, said: "You may be going to Switzerland soon, N3. Not on a pleasure jaunt, naturally, so you won't need your climbing boots and alpenstock."

I always enjoyed these brief sessions with the boss of AXE. When action was not imminent there was time for a little banter and repartee.

I grinned at this gaunt, stiff man—our relationship was very nearly that of father and son—and said: "I've already climbed the Matterhorn, sir. Years ago. Anyway, it's old hat now. Maybe this time I can do Monte Rosa or the Breithorn."

Hawk held up a lean, wizened hand. "Spare me the details of your achievements, please! I know most of them, anyway—at least those done on the perpendicular. Your horizontal feats don't interest me unless they interfere with your work. Anyway, you've got to get through Purg again before you go anywhere. You're due in a couple of weeks, aren't you?"

Indeed I was. Purg, short for purgatory, was the brief but intensive refresher course that every AXE agent must undergo once a year. The name was indicative of its purpose and importance. While undergoing Purg, an agent literally hovered between heaven and hell. Between another year of active duty and retirement on a pension. If you could cut the mustard—and the mustard was thick and sticky and hot—then you went back to duty. If you failed, you were out. Forever! You went outside!

Hawk had regarded me speculatively. "I hope you make it this time, son. I want you on this job. It may turn out to be easy, a big nothing—on the other hand it could turn out to be a real hell-buster!"

So in due course I had gone to Purg. It was as hot and miserable and tough as ever. Purg was, in fact, a quasi-hell somewhere in the arid wastes of the American South-west. Not even I knew exactly where it was. No agent did. The secrecy shrouding Purg was merely another facet of the AXE policy that no agent ever be told more than was necessary for him to do his job. Purg itself taught some of the most refined and up-to-date tortures—and if Purg knew them, the enemy would know them! And, as Purg well knew, the agent did not live who could resist torture forever.

Purg was run by a special unlimited fund. Even Congress did not know where the money went. And if any member of that august body could have seen the cluster of blistering tin huts in which Purg was conducted, he might have doubted the wisdom of the money spent, and of Purg itself. But Purg knew! The courses and procedures taught in that thirsty squalor kept AXE agents alive. Nearly all of them.

So I was taken to Purg in the usual draped and sealed car, and my personal hell began. No women, no song, no wine. Even water was rationed. No *dolce vita* was Purg! You were up at dawn and you didn't stop till dusk. Calisthenics that would kill an ordinary man; endless obstacle courses; thirty-mile hikes over desert with one pint of water and packs filled with stones. Endless hours on the firing range with everything from derringers to machine guns. Rope-climbing to strengthen the arms and shoulders—and nearly tear them from their sockets. Judo and karate. Knots—seemingly millions of knots, everything from the magnus hitch to the double sheet bight.

This year, for the first time, there had been *savate,* the French form of foot boxing. My jaw had ached for weeks afterward from being kicked.

Then there were the long sessions inside the steaming tin barracks. Courses in the slang and argot of the world, even Cockney rhyming slang. Code, cipher, cryptology. Radio sending and receiving. Instruction in the use of, and defense against, sword canes, blowguns, pressure pistols. Purg had a Black Museum that made Scotland Yard's look like a child's collection.

Actual fighting with clubs and wooden swords and brass knuckles and trench knives—fights that were not called off by the instructor until the last possible second before serious injury. Minor injuries were not taken into account, and of bloodshed there was plenty.

One day, shortly before the end of the course, I was taken into an airless hut for a private briefing. My instructor was a brawny young man in a T-shirt and ragged jeans. His fine teeth gleamed whitely against his incredible tan as he told me to sit down. The hut contained two hard chairs and a deal table.

"You're getting a break, N3," the instructor said. "Getting to sit down, I mean. I'm glad for both of us."

I sank into the chair with a sigh of genuine weariness. Purg tried even me. Like every top AXE agent, I had a good measure of resourcefulness, courage, and determination. And no scruples. Purg tested them all to the breaking point.

I signed for and lit one of my three daily cigarettes. "What's it all about? Whatever it is—I'm happy about it. This chair beats a thirty-mile hike with a hundred pounds of rocks."

The instructor nodded. "I agree. So let's get to it. This is a very special briefing on two rather odd subjects— Swiss banks and French keys. That mean anything to you? It doesn't to me, but I've been briefed on those things, and I'm to pass it on to you."

"I think I can guess," I conceded, thinking of Hawk and his mention of a possible upcoming mission in Switzerland. I drew deeply on my cigarette, savoring it. "Yes, I think I know what it's about. Not much, but a little. So let's get with it, shall we? What the hell is a French key?"

The instructor grinned. "Not so fast. We're getting the cart before the horse, I think." He opened a drawer in the table and took out a sheaf of papers and what looked like an oversized bankbook. The man rifled through the papers for a moment, then leaned back, put his feet on the table and looked quizzically at me. "Just how much do you know about Swiss banks and banking methods?"

"Damned little," I admitted. "What everyone knows, I suppose. That most of the shady money in the world is deposited in Swiss banks. It's protected by Swiss law so that nobody but the rightful owners—hah—can get at it. I've heard, and read, that the Swiss people as a whole are just about as honest as they come, but their banking system has been known to drive honest cops nuts all over the world. Not even Interpol has been able to crack it. Any dictator, gangster, gunrunner, dope seller, white slaver—you name it—can stash his money away in a Swiss bank and no one can touch it. No one but him."

The instructor nodded. He lit another cigarette and I watched with envy. I had one more to last me all day. The young man grinned at me and waved the smoke in my direction. "Be thankful, N3. At least you can smell it. The others can't even do that."

"Thanks a lot," I said bitterly. "Go on, Torquemada! Get on with the Swiss banking bit."

"Okay," the instructor agreed cheerfully. He glanced at his papers again. "What you *do* know about Swiss banking is substantially correct. It's a hard nut to crack. In fact, it can't be cracked—it never has been cracked!"

Until now, I thought, a little resentfully. I'll bet Hawk expects *me* to crack it!

"There are a couple of prime reasons," the instructor said, "why the Swiss system can't be cracked. One is because it's so damned *legal!* The secrecy of the banks is protected by the Swiss constitution. Not even the Swiss Government can force a bank to disclose the name of a depositor, the amount to his credit, or a record of his deposits and withdrawals. If the government tried to pry into those things, they'd probably start a revolution. If any other country did it the Swiss Army would probably fight. So you see, it's a sort of a national conspiracy."

I nodded agreement. "A rigged deal if ever I saw one. Loaded dice." I was getting curiouser and curiouser, like Alice in Wonderland. What in hell did Hawk want from me—steal a few million to tide the U.S. Treasury over?

My instructor grinned. "Okay. But that's only half the story. To make it even tougher, the Swiss banks, mostly in Geneva and Berne, use secret codes to identify their depositors. These accounts are so closely guarded that— and get this—nothing is ever put down on paper. Code numbers are always memorized."

"How the hell? I can understand a depositor remembering his own code number, but how can a bank manager—?"

"Easy." They just have a lot of bank managers, and assistants. Each one has only a few clients. It isn't hard. Anyone can memorize, say, ten simple numbers. And they *can* be simple if only two people know them. The thing gets a little more complex when it comes to authenticating telegraphic payments, delivery of documents, or dispatch of important information." He was reading from the papers in his hand now.

"Get this, N3. The test number—this is *not* the memorized code number—the *test* number is compiled by *adding* the permanent code number to the date on which the telegram is dispatched, plus the number, or numbers, appearing last in the New York Stock Market closing report on the day before the telegram is sent." The instructor leaned back and grinned.

All I could say was, "Whew!"

"Whew is right. When the Swiss say their banks are the most secure in the world they aren't exactly whistling Dixie. And that ain't all, N3."

I groaned. "You mean there's more?"

"There is." The instructor reached into the table drawer again. "There is the French key. This little gadget.

Here, take a look and I'll explain how it works." He tossed the little steel rod to me.

I examined it carefully. It was a little thicker than an ordinary swizzle stick and about as long. I tapped it on my chair. It rang with a shrill, musical sound.

"It doesn't look like a key to me," I said. "What does it lock? Or unlock?"

"Nothing. It isn't supposed to. In fact, the French key is a little old-fashioned now. It isn't used much any more. But it's to be included in your briefing. This is how it works.

"This so-called key takes the place of the memorized code number. It is usually used when a fair-sized vault is rented. Not just a safe-deposit box. This rod, or key, fits into a special hole in the center of the vault lock. After the vault is locked, in the presence of the client and the bank manager, the French key is wedged into the hole. Then it is cut off, by a very special saw that leaves special markings on the two ends of the key. Part of the key remains in the lock. The other half is taken away by the client. The vault will only be opened when the two parts of the key are matched again, dovetailed. Each key is cut with a special saw that is then destroyed. No two keys are ever the same. You see the result?"

"I do indeed," I said. "The only guy who can have that particular vault opened is the guy with that particular key. Of course, he could give it to someone else. Or it could be stolen."

"So he could," said the instructor. "And so it could." He stood up and stretched. "And knowing something, not much, but something, of what you AXE characters are usually up to, I dare say that stealing, or killing, or some such skullduggery, is probably at the bottom of all this. Anyway, you've had your lecture on Swiss banking and the French key. I hope I haven't bored you?"

"It still beats hiking thirty miles with rocks on my back," I admitted.

And so I had once again come through the hazards of Purg. I graduated at the top of the class, as I had expected to do—there is nothing of false modesty about me—and after the final parachute jump I had been set free. Hawk had even let me enjoy a few days slaking the biggest thirst west of Suez and catching up on my bed time. Both with and without girls. I had then drawn a couple of minor assignments, always with the sense of marking time.

One day Hawk had sent for me. In the briefing room hidden somewhere in the huge complex of the AXE central offices—these snuggling behind the false front of the Amalgamated Press and Wire Service on Dupont Circle in Washington, D.C.—I had received an entire day of the most intensive briefing I could remember. Next day I was on my way. And now here I was.

Yes. Here I was. But where in hell *was* I?

Still alias Mr. Frank Manning of Cleveland, I gazed in perplexity at the tall wall of crumbling red brick that confronted me. An instant later, I realized what had happened. I was in an *impasse*. I had been so lost in my own thoughts that I had taken a wrong turn somewhere. Mr. Manning cursed mildly, took off his so American hat to scratch his so American head, and smiled meekly at the old woman who was plucking chickens in the window of a *boucherie* across the street. The crone gave me a toothless smile in return and wagged her head knowingly. These *touristes Americains* were hopeless, forever strolling into dead ends!

Mr. Manning turned back the way he had come, trotting nervously over the narrow cobbled way, as though ashamed of such a gaffe, his little rubber belly swaying before him. The streets were beginning to fill now with busy Genevese going about their daily routine. People no longer paid much attention to the pudgy American. Bikes and small cars clanged and honked at me. The sun was half an hour higher now, dappling even the narrowest lanes with limpid gold that bore little warmth. A first hint of autumn was in the breeze skirling in from Lac Léman.

I let Mr. Frank Manning play his role automatically, while I went back to my own thoughts—the thoughts of KILLMASTER. As I emerged from the cul-de-sac, I glanced at the very special AXE watch on my wrist. Probably the finest watch in the world, and it was mildly amusing to remember that it had been made right here in Geneva. They cost a thousand dollars apiece, these AXE watches, and the Swiss never knew for whom they were making them.

The watch told me that I had been on the march for twenty-five minutes. Two or three more and I would be back at the Hotel Lux.

It turned out to be exactly two minutes. The fat American gentleman ambled around a corner into the Allée de Napoléon, surely a grandiose name for such a dreary slum street, then halted abruptly. Swiftly, but in no way betraying shock or alarm, I turned to gaze into the window of a small secondhand book store. The character of Mr. Manning evaporated. Nick Carter took over, every sense, every finely honed reaction quivering and alert. There were watchers in front of the Hotel Lux.

There were two of them. Bulky men in dark raincoats and soft felt hats. They were leaning indolently against a bare wooden fence across from the hotel, smoking and gazing with sullen boredom at the dismal façade.

I pretended to study a pile of dusty medical tomes in the shop window. My breathing quickened and I felt the familiar thrill of anticipation run through me, accompanied by a tiny razor of fear. Healthy fear. An animal intimation of danger, a hundredfold stronger than the average man's, that was my warning device. It had saved my life countless times.

Not police! In a flashing instant, my brain examined that possibility and discarded it. They did not look like police. There was no reason why they *should* be police.

The papers of the Herr Rubli Kurz had been in perfec order. The half-drunken night porter who had taken my money—in advance, please—had been just another dere-lict, though well dressed, who would be gone in a few hours. Nothing to worry about. He had handed me a key and gone back to snore on his couch.

I began to edge back around the corner from which I had just come. I edged sideways, a foot at a time, keeping my right eye fixed on the two watchers. I saw one of them glance in my direction. Inside the flabby body of Mr. Manning, I tensed and waited. If they had spotted me, if the girl *had* indeed fingered me, it would be as Kurz. Not as Frank Manning. Yet you never knew.

The man who had glanced at me flipped his cigarette butt into the gutter and spat. He said something to his companion. They both laughed, then resumed their bored watch of the Hotel Lux.

I slipped around the corner. The guise of Mr. Manning was dropping away fast now. I quickened my pace, all but running, heading for the little *allée* that ran behind the Hotel. I had noticed it from the window, earlier.

The girl, the Baroness von Stadt, was still in that dingy hotel room. Still bound and gagged. Possibly still out cold. If she was on the level, she was in terrible danger. If not—then I had to know that, too! Because if the watchers weren't police they could only be the minions of Max Rader or Shikoku Hondo. Or both. Presumably both were in Geneva by now, and might already have joined forces.

I turned the corner into the *allée* and began to run. I turned a valve on the rubber stomach and let the air whistle out. The thing got in the way.

As I ran, I checked my three constant and faithful companions. Wilhelmina, the stripped-down Luger, was secure in the plastic holster inside my belt; Hugo, the snake-deadly stiletto was ready in my sleeve; Pierre, the lethal gas pellet, awaited the call for duty in my pocket. Still running, I considered which to use, if I had to use any of them. I hoped I wouldn't. Wilhelmina made noise, which was bad if you didn't want to attract attention. And a strange hotel room was no place to be tossing poison gas about. It would have to be Hugo, then. As silent and as deadly as a fer-de-lance.

I took the high fence behind the Hotel Lux in a single lunge, leaping and grabbing and legging myself over in one fluid motion. I might be mistaken, I conceded as I made my way across the littered back yard. I might be seeing danger when there was none—yet. Maybe the men were only watchers after all. Maybe there was no one inside. But I didn't think I was wrong. My senses were sounding an alarm. Warning of danger for the girl, for myself, for both of us. And my warning system was very rarely at fault.

I went up the rusty fire escape in a silent, writhing climb. Now that the rubber belly was gone the clothes of Mr. Manning bagged grotesquely around me. As I approached the window of my room, I slowed just a trifle, crouched, and glided the last few feet as silently as a tiger stalking a meal. Cautiously, I peered through dirt-fogged glass into the room. My lips tightened at what I saw. The Baroness von Stadt was in danger. But it was not the sort of danger that I had expected.

Mr. Shikoku Hondo, late of Tokyo Prison, was no gentleman. He stood now in the dingy room, staring down at the still unconscious girl on the sofa. He licked his lips and his mouth opened, disclosing a slightly bucktoothed leer of appreciation. I could almost hear the little vermin hissing to himself: "Ah, yes! So beautiful! So lovely! Yesss—and so helpless! She will not even know of this thing I am about to do. Ah, yes!"

Then Hondo seemed to think of something. He went to the door of the room and locked it. I might have known, I thought. The lock wasn't much to begin with.

And I wasn't the only guy with a Lock-picker's Special

Hondo came back to stand before the girl. He never bothered to glance at the window. He was much too intent on his urgent business for that. From my vantage point, Hondo resembled nothing so much as a thin, graying, saffron-faced monkey in a neat business suit.

Hondo went closer to the sleeping girl. The Baroness von Stadt had been tossing in her sleep, apparently, because her skirt had ridden well up on her thighs. Now Hondo leaned down and kissed each well-displayed white thigh. If there had ever been any doubt of Hondo's intention in my mind, it vanished now. I tensed and made ready for action, yet still held my fire. Let the little ape enjoy himself while he could. That wouldn't be long. And no real harm could come to the girl. I glanced around and below swiftly. The back area was quiet. Nobody had spotted me crouching on the fire escape. The men in front must still be waiting for Hondo to complete his business and leave the hotel.

But Mr. Shikoku Hondo was a man who believed in mixing business with pleasure. He was kneeling before the girl now, his small eyes feasting on her flesh as he unfastened the straps about her ankles. I grinned. Surely Hondo must be wondering who had tied the girl, had left her drugged and bound?

No. I was wrong. At the moment Hondo was intent on only one thing—ravishing a lovely girl who could not defend herself. Who ordinarily would never have deigned to look at him. Would have spit on him!

Anger began to well up in me. I had hardly expected Hondo to be a paragon of virtue. Very few of my customers were. But this was a new low in human depravity. Ravishing a sleeping girl!

Hondo had completed his task of untying the girl's ankles now. He flung the straps aside. I could see the spittle drooling down his chin.

Hondo gently spread-eagled the girl onto the sofa, ar-

ranging the long beige-and-white legs into a wide-flung
V. He was in no hurry, this monkey-man. He moved
almost reluctantly, savoring every instant of his approaching pleasure. Watching him, I couldn't help being reminded of the Japanese legend of the monkey who came
to the princess in the night. Hondo's movements quickened at last. He had tugged the Baroness' skirt up around
her waist. My muscles began to surge into readiness. Perhaps, I admitted to myself, I had let it go on so long
because of the immense pleasure I was going to derive
from cheating this crummy little bastard!

Hondo fumbled with the front of his trousers. He
stepped between the girl's wide-flung legs and bent to the
last and most pleasant of his tasks. He hooked his skinny
fingers into the waistband of a pair of very skimpy black
panties.

I had long known how to go through a glass window
without badly injuring myself. I backed away, half
turned my back to the window, and went through it
like a relentless and avenging battering ram.

Four

Everything happened at once!

Hondo whirled with a hissing scream of surprise and fear, his slanty eyes as wide as they could ever be. One scrawny yellow claw grabbed for the back of his neck, as if he had a sudden itch there.

Knife! I thought. Neck scabbard! Obviously Hondo wanted as little noise as possible. On that one thing we agreed.

Hugo was ready in my sleeve, but I decided I did not need the stiletto. Hondo was surprised, in panic. He would miss, throwing at my feint.

I leaped at Hondo, then abruptly braked and slid to one side. As I did so, I saw the girl's eyes open. Saw her straining to scream her terror through the gag.

Hondo fell for the feint. The throwing knife buzzed through the air where I had been. Hondo was slow in recovering from the throw. He was off balance. Thinking what a fine opportunity this was to use my recently acquired *savate,* I took three steps toward the now cringing Hondo. I leaped into the air, turned my back, and kicked hard at Hondo's groin.

As my iron-shod heel slammed into the most tender part of Hondo's anatomy, I grinned and said, "So solly, Mr. Moto!"

Hondo screamed in anguish. Slime spewed from his gaping mouth. He folded in the middle, slowly, grabbing with both hands at his ruined genitals. His eyes bugged from a face that was now more green than yellow. He fell to the floor, and, still jackknifed, still screaming and clawing at himself, began to thrash about like a snake that has been cut in half.

Over Hondo's screams, I heard a thudding sound. I glanced at the sofa. The girl, still gagged, with her hands still bound, had fallen to the floor. Her lovely face was distorted with fear, her eyes wide with the terror she had awakened to. She tried to get up, failed, and fell back with another thud, her long white legs waving in the air.

One thing at a time. The Baroness could wait a couple of seconds. Thank God for the gag, I thought as I leaped for the groveling Hondo. She can probably scream louder than Hondo!

As it was, the joint was going to be jumping with cops any minute. I reached down and grabbed Hondo as though he were a sack of flour. This was a chance to get one of my enemies out of the way, right off the bat, and I wasn't the man to pass up such an opportunity.

The frail Hondo put hardly any strain on my shoulders and back as I carried him to the shattered window. Even in his agony, Hondo sensed my intention and began to struggle and claw at me.

I braced myself, swung him back and forth twice, then hurled him out of the open window.

I saw the thin body catch and hang for a moment on the railing of the fire escape. Hondo tried to grab for the rusty iron, failed, and plunged to the back court, still screaming.

I turned my attention back to the Baroness von Stadt. Not a moment to waste now.

She had succeeded in getting to her feet. She started to back away from me, but I pushed her roughly back on the sofa and pinned her there. She stared up at me, her dark gray eyes blurred with hysteria.

"Listen," I snapped. "Listen fast! I'm Carter of AXE.

Nick Carter! You're all right now. You're safe. Do you understand?"

There was no comprehension in her deep eyes. She struggled fiercely, trying to drive a shapely knee into me.

"I'm sorry," I told her. "I hate to do this, but there's no time." I slapped her hard across the face, leaving a crimson imprint. The girl gave a moan, audible even through the gag, and fell back on the sofa.

I grabbed her by the ears and thrust my face close to hers. "Listen, goddamn it! You've got to understand. The police will be here any minute. I'm Nick Carter of AXE! You picked me up on the boat last night. Never mind how I look now! I'm in disguise! Just listen hard. I'm Nick Carter and you're the Baroness von Stadt and we're supposed to work together on Mission Tiger! You got it?"

Goddamn it anyway, I thought. Goddamn Hawk! And double goddamn working with a woman!

But the slap had done the trick. Sanity came flooding back into the gray eyes. Suddenly she relaxed and nodded.

"Thank God," I said. I unfastened her hands, working as fast as I could. Time was running short. I couldn't understand why the cops weren't already there, stolid and complacent and very efficient in their own bumbling way: "Monsieur and mademoiselle were perhaps having the friendly party, *non?* But yes! We understand perfectly. The Hotel Lux has had such complaints before. But yes! But the noise, Monsieur? *Formidable!!* And who is to explain the body in the back court, Monsieur?"

I yanked the gag from the girl's mouth, not bothering to be gentle. She gasped and recoiled from me, doubt once more filling her eyes. "Are you—are you really Nicholas Carter? I don't know—I—I'm so confused!"

I yanked up my coat sleeve, tore at my shirt, and showed her the tiny AXE symbol tattooed on my inner elbow. "See that? I'm Nick Carter, all right. No more time for yakking now! Get yourself together, for God's sake. Your clothes, purse, shoes, whatever. We've got to run for it.

Hondo had a couple of bully boys outside. I don't think they'll bother us now, but the cops will. We've got to run, woman, RUN!"

All the time I talked I was moving swiftly around the little room, not wasting a motion. Retrieving the rhino-hide suitcase, tossing the straps and gag into it, my glance roving the room for anything that might give the police a clue. Or Hondo's men. Or Max Rader's men. Or both. Everyone was against us now. Join AXE and work alone, I thought savagely as I emptied an ashtray into the suit-case.

Behind me I could hear the girl straightening her clothes, rustling and swishing, breathing heavily. Sud-denly I heard her gasp. I whirled, saw her with her dress up high, straightening her stockings. She had halted in mid-act and was staring at the empty little garter holsters. "Never mind that *now*," I said. "Your little friends are safe! I've got them in here." I patted Gladstone.

The Baroness dropped her skirt and stared at me, her face crimson. "Yes," I said, brutal in my impatience, "I saw your pretty legs! Very nice. Now get moving!" I gave her a brusque push toward the door. "Unlock it and wait for me in the hall. I'll be right there. And get your track shoes on, baby, because I've got a feeling our luck is run-ning out."

I heard the door latch click. Dashing for the tiny bath-room, I took a last look around. Nothing. I ran back into the room and was about to snatch up the suitcase when I saw something on the floor in a corner. What the hell?

I leaped for the object and scooped it up. False teeth! An upper plate, for God's sake. Even in the exigency of the moment, I had to laugh. Hondo's false teeth. Must have come out with the first spew of vomit.

Gladstone was securely fastened. No time to open it. I dropped the false teeth into my pocket and ran for the door.

Baroness von Stadt was waiting just outside. She held a finger to her lips. "I think I hear someone coming up the stairs. Do you think it's the police?"

"It won't be the little old winemaker," I snapped. "Come on! Run on your toes."

Lugging the heavy suitcase, I ran down the dim, musty-smelling corridor toward the stairs. I stopped just before I reached the landing, signaling the girl to halt behind me. I peered cautiously over the railing, down the stairwell.

Too late! Two flights below us the concierge was toiling upward, puffing and complaining in voluble French. Behind him I saw the flat caps of two *agents de police*. The concierge was busily explaining that he ran a respectable hotel and couldn't understand what was going on.

Wait until they find the body in the back yard, Buster! I reached for the girl and pulled her across the landing.

"Can't go down," I whispered. "We'll have to go up and pray for a way out on the roof. Quickly now, and no noise."

I made the girl go first, pushing her ahead of me, rushing her, afraid she would stumble in her high heels and give us away. We would have a few minutes, at best, while the cops puzzled over the empty room and the wrecked window.

Three flights up, the stairs ended. But I saw the glint of a skylight and ran toward it, my hopes soaring. Maybe the mice could escape the trap after all.

When I saw the skylight, though, my hopes fell again. It was incredibly old, rusty, and grimy. About four by six, pushing a little tent of glass above the roof level. There was no ladder about, and the skylight was a good ten feet above my head. That in itself was no great problem—I'm over six feet tall—but there was no hand-hold up there. No dangling chain or rope. Nothing but an expanse of cloudy glass and rust-corroded hinges. I cursed. Was this another cul-de-sac? The final one?

I did not doubt that I could handle the Swiss cops if they trapped me. Even with the girl, though it would make it tougher. But only as a last, desperate resort did I want to tangle with the police. It was an ironclad dictum at AXE—never, never, *never* get involved with the police. Hawk continually repeated it.

I grinned bitterly. Wish Hawk were here now. I could stand on his shoulders.

Then I saw it, on the bilious-colored wall. A fire hose on a reel. Even a Z-rated hotel like the Lux had to have fire hoses. It was ancient, brittle, coiled like a dead and rotted snake, but maybe it would do. Next to it, in a glass-fronted box, was an alarm key.

The Baroness was watching me, breathing hard, her eyes wide, one hand clasping a breast. I stood the rhino-hide suitcase on end beneath the center of the skylight. "Steady it," I commanded. "Hold it so I don't fall!"

I leaped for the fire hose, dragged it squealing and complaining off the reel. With the heavy brass nozzle in my hand, I stepped onto the upended suitcase. The top arch of the skylight was now only about three feet over my head. I looked down at the girl. She was on her knees beside the suitcase, struggling to hold it steady under my weight.

I grinned at her. "Good girl! Now, this is going to make a hell of a lot of noise! We've got to move fast, because those cops are going to be up here on the double. I'm going to smash the glass, hook the hose over the iron sash, and bring it down again. Then you'll have to climb up and out on the roof. Fast! Think you can do it?"

"I—I don't know. I'm not very strong. I'll try."

"Trying won't cut it," I said harshly. "You've got to *do* it!" This was what it was like, working with a woman! But no time for that now. Time! We needed more time, and—my eyes went to the fire alarm beside the hose reel.

We needed time *and* a distraction, a diversion. Maybe—just maybe!

I leaped off the suitcase and began tearing off my coat. I dropped it on the floor and ripped off my shirt. The conservative white dress shirt of Mr. Frank Manning. RIP!

The Baroness von Stadt eyed my chest and shoulders. "What in the world—"

"The oldest *trick* in the world," I told her. "Creating a little diversion for our friends downstairs." I shrugged back into my coat and picked up the ripped shirt. I pulled the girl to her feet and pushed her toward the fire alarm box. "When I drop this shirt down the stairwell, you push that button—and pray the damned thing still works."

She nodded. Before I had taken a dozen steps, she called softly after me: "Nicholas! I—I can't get the box open. It's rusted shut!"

I came swiftly back and saw that she was right. I patted her shoulder. "Good kid! Glad you tested it. Stand back now."

I wrapped the shirt around my fist and smashed into the box. Glass tinkled.

I looked at her. "Remember. When I drop the shirt, be ready to move!"

I ran on tiptoe down the corridor to the stairwell and peered cautiously over. Nothing, though I could hear faint voices.

This will give them something else to chatter about, I thought, taking my cigarette lighter from my coat pocket.

I held the tattered shirt at arm's length and lit the tail. The cloth took but a moment to catch. Then flame leaped toward my hand and the acrid smell of smoke began to fill the hallway. I glanced back at the girl. Her finger was poised at the alarm box. I dropped the flaming shirt down the stairwell. It drifted slowly, blazing and smoking like an exploded balloon.

As I ran back along the corridor, I heard the gratifying clang of a fire gong somewhere in the recesses of the building. Thank God! The thing worked. Now, with any luck at all, we had a little time. But only a little!

Ten seconds later, I was again on the suitcase, swinging the brass nozzle like a mace at the skylight. It shattered at first impact. I swung the nozzle again and again, working amid a shower of glass, shielding my eyes, feeling a nick of pain now and then, hearing the continuing clang of the fire alarm.

In a minute I had smashed the glass from one entire side of the skylight. I swung the nozzle over a rusted sash, caught it, and leaped down. I twisted the hose a couple of times and tied it in a knot at the bottom.

I turned to the girl. "On my back, quick. Put your arms around my neck and hang on tight! We're going up!"

Her arms, soft and sweet-smelling, locked around my neck. I could feel the swell of her breasts and hear the panting of soft breath. Her body exuded the barest hint of perfume, subtle, evanescent, blending with her own flesh smell.

I went up the hose hand over hand, climbing like a homesick angel. I hooked one arm over the sash and with the other hand pushed the girl up and out onto the roof. Her posterior was soft-firm against my thrust. I grinned. Sorry, lady. No time for the niceties just now.

The Baroness' high heels came off and tumbled past my face. Over me she said, "Damn!" At first I thought it was because of the shoes, but then I saw that her skirt was caught on one of the rusty hinges. She was scrambling and kicking, trying to free herself, still cursing. Soft little panting curses that went from English to French into German.

"Hold still," I commanded. "I'll get it. This is no time to be modest."

I had to pull her skirt high to disentangle it. Finally it came loose. I put one hand against the bottom of black lace panties and shoved hard. "Out you go!"

She shot out of the skylight like a champagne cork. I heard her gasp and curse again as she landed.

I chuckled as I slid down the hose. Any girl who could swear like that had been around! Baroness she might be, but she had not led a sheltered life!

Our luck was holding. As I gathered up the rhino-hide bag, I heard the alarm still ringing. There was shouting below stairs now. I grinned. The cops must think they had stumbled into a yo-yo academy. Now if we could just find Hondo's body, we would have plenty of time.

Holding Gladstone in one hand, I went back up the hose, using my legs this time. I propped the suitcase on the edge of the skylight and peered out. The girl was straddling the roof peak, facing me, her honey hair in wild disorder, her lovely face dirty and flushed from exertion. She blinked at me. "Nicholas! This—this roof! How do we get down?"

I looked around. It *would* be a problem. It was a mansard roof, the ancient leads as slippery and treacherous as shale, the sides sloping steeply away from the peak. Like being stranded on top of a whale.

"Just hold on tight," I told her. "We'll be all right. Not afraid, are you?"

To my surprise, her red mouth widened in a smile. Dubious, but still a smile. In her soft, slurred, and very faintly accented English, she said: "Frankly, I'm terrified! I've never been *through* anything like this before. But never mind—what do we *do?*"

Quite a girl. My heart—at least what an AXE man had to use for a heart—began to warm to her. I began to hope that she really was on the level, that Hawk was right about her. Perched there astride the ridge of the Hotel Lux, shoeless, disheveled, her skirt up around her thighs, she made a lovely, if slightly improbable, picture.

I couldn't resist the quip, even at this moment of hurry and danger. "You know, Baroness, this is quite an experience for me. I've never seen a member of the nobility in exactly your position before."

The smile vanished and was quickly replaced by hauteur. "I do not appreciate your humor, Nicholas. Please get us out of this. Won't the police be coming to inspect the roof soon? They are not stupid, you know."

"I know. You're right, of course." I glanced past her to the end of the ridge. "Start moving backward. Just scoot along like you were a kid playing games. We've got to see what's at the end of this ridge."

I followed her along the ridge, keeping a firm hold on Gladstone. I sure as hell couldn't afford to lose Gladstone. Better the girl than that precious bag. An ungallant thought, I know, but at that moment it was the truth.

At the end of the roof peak I managed to edge around the girl to see what lay beyond. I was sweating just a little, and not entirely from the exertion. A lot depended on what lay below. If we were trapped there we would be sitting ducks for the police, who could cover us from the skylight and force us back. Not even I could fight odds like that, especially with the girl's life also at stake. I didn't mind risking my own life—I did it every day— and I didn't mind risking *hers* on a fifty-fifty chance, but with no chance it would be murder!

I peeked out over the end of the building. Only ten feet below was the flat roof of the adjacent house. I took a deep breath and jumped.

The flat tarred roof felt good under my feet. I looked up and held out my arms. "Come on, baby. Jump for it. I've got you."

She came fluttering down like an exquisite, slightly rumpled doll. I caught her lightly in my arms. For a moment her pliant body clung to mine. I kissed her lightly on the lips.

The Baroness von Stadt pulled herself away from me

She stared at me, her eyes wide, her color high. Smudges of dirt on her face enhanced her beauty.

"Don't be angry. It was only a medal kiss."

"A medal kiss?"

"Yeah. For being such a brave kid. You did all right, you know. But let's get going. There's a fire escape over there. Let's take it down, shall we? Fast." I picked up Gladstone.

She hobbled beside me. "Owww—my feet. This gravel —my shoes fell off, you know." She halted abruptly and stared at me in dismay. "Nicholas! My shoes! How can I—I mean, I, we'll attract all sorts of attention. Me walking through the streets with no shoes. In middle September."

I took a shoe from each coat pocket and handed them to her. "Be my guest. Courtesy of AXE. We strive to please. Now for God's sake put them on and let's get cracking. I don't want to press our luck."

She balanced herself, a shapely hand on my shoulder, as she wriggled her toes into the shoes. "Yes," she murmured, "we have had a lot of luck haven't we? Maybe we're lucky for each other? Do you think?" She shot me a sidelong glance.

"I only think one thing," I said. *"Move!"* I shoved her toward the fire escape. It led down to a narrow *allée*. There was no one about.

I motioned the Baroness down. "You first. We're on the run now, but we may still have a chance. Hondo's body will keep them busy for awhile. And Hondo's men will probably be scurrying back to report to Max Rader. We've got a breathing spell. First thing to do is to find a hidey hole somewhere and sort a few things out. We've got a lot to talk about, you and I."

Just before the Baroness began to descend the fire escape she looked up at me. "I wasn't angry, you know."

I frowned. "What are you talking about?"

"About the medal. It's the nicest medal I've ever gotten."

As I followed her down the iron ladder, I thought of Hawk's admonition: the Baroness von Stadt is an agent, temporarily working for AXE. She will be treated in such manner—etc, etc. . . .

That order might be just a little hard to obey.

Five

"Mein Gott," said the Baroness von Stadt, lapsing into German for the first time since we had met, if you didn't count the curses on the roof of the Hotel Lux. *"Mein Gott,"* she repeated. "I never really suspected that such crazy things can happen! Fantastic! *Formidable!* As you Yanks say—out of this world!"

I glanced around the small workingman's bistro where, at the moment, we were having chocolate and brioches. There was a sailor at a table near the bar staring morosely into his glass, and a couple of laboring types at the bar itself, but no one was paying any attention to us—which was just as well. The Baroness had repaired some of the damage to her clothes, and might pass in a crowd, but I—or Frank Manning, if you pleased—was a mess! My hair wasn't bad, cut *en brosse* as it was, but my face was cut in several places, I was shirtless, and the business suit was beginning to show both dirt and wear. Without the rubber belly, which I had long since thrown away, it sagged.

Still, our entrance had aroused no particular interest in the little bistro. The Coq d'Or, it seemed, was accustomed to rough types.

I glanced at my AXE watch. I found it hard to believe that it was only a quarter of nine in the morning. A gold and blue morning in mid-September, with Lac Léman spread before us as placid as a sheet of glass.

I reached across the little table to pat the girl's hand.

50

"As I said before, you did real well! But my boss told me that you've worked with Bonn for a long time—so why all the amazement? If you've been an agent, I mean—"

She squeezed my fingers, then took her hand away. "Never anything like this, Nicholas. My God, no! I have worked for Bonn a long time, yes, but I soon began to think it was dull. Actually dull. So much routine, so much paperwork. Many times I have been on the verge of quitting, throwing it all up, but then I would consider that I was serving my country, in the only way I could— and so I stayed. But this—" She laughed suddenly and reached for my hand again and held it.

"I repeat—I have never seen anything like it." Her hand tightened on mine. "I have never seen anything like you either, my Nicholas! You were *magnifique!* I begin to believe the legends I have heard about you."

I frowned. That was the trouble with being a legend. Too many people knew about you.

I finished my chocolate and glanced around again. Nothing to fret about. I pulled the sagging coat tighter around myself. I *did* look like a bum. If a stray cop wandered in, there might be some embarrassing questions.

"Baroness," I said, "finish your chocolate and bun. We've got to get the hell out of here. I don't know where, but I'll try to think of something." Actually, I thought, our only chance was to get to the *dépôt* before either the cops, or Hondo's men, or Rader's, caught up with us. I really ought to talk to Hawk again anyway, tell him that Hondo was dead and that the game was getting blazing hot.

Time was wasting. Max Rader might be at the small private bank of Paul Chardet et Fils this very moment— might be presenting the French key and opening the vault and taking out the golden tiger with the ruby eyes.

Hawk always covered every angle, of course. Other agents were watching the bank in shifts—but that had been set up before they knew about Max Rader's face job. The pix they had were useless now, as Hawk had so grimly pointed out.

Every possible way out of the country was being guarded too, but it was hard to seal off an entire country. Anything could go wrong. And if Rader tried to shoot his way out, which he probably would, that meant getting nasty blood on the pretty Swiss scenery. They wouldn't like that. Anyway, if an AXE man got in a jam, he was strictly on his own. Officially, at least. The U.S. Government wouldn't touch you with a ten-foot pole. You smelled strictly of skunk!

Goddamn it, I thought, I've got to do *something*. Fast. I can't just sit here holding hands with the Baroness.

The Baroness! This nubile and now so friendly and trusting woman across the table from me. I had a million questions to ask her, wanting to catch her in one lie. Hawk might accept her. Bonn might swear on a stack of Bibles that she was kosher. Not me, though. Not yet. I was still suspicious of the way she had picked me up on the boat the night before.

But all that could wait. Right now I had to—

The Baroness patted my hand. "You are pensive, my Nicholas. It is because you do not trust me. That is true, is it not?"

The soft slur of words, the faintest of Germanic intonations, the too perfect English of the foreigner. She talked like a highly educated woman. Her picture and passport matched. Hawk and Bonn vouched for her. She must really *be* the Baroness Elizabeth von Stadt. Then why couldn't I accept her? Maybe I was getting AXE-happy! Rocks in my head. Maybe I should have flunked Purg and retired!

"Is it not?" she repeated. Funny, I thought. She must be thirty, at least. She looks tired at times, tired and worn. And still I think of her as a girl.

"It must be that," she insisted. "That is why you drugged me. Why you searched me as I slept."

I stared hard at her. She colored. She had the very fair skin of the Nordic. Now it was pink.

"That was routine," I said. I hadn't told her of what Hondo tried to do to her. She had awakened too late to understand Hondo's intent, had only seen the fight without understanding it. I did not intend to tell her the truth. A nasty secret best kept to myself. The Baroness said she did not know Hondo. Had never seen him before. Did not know how he fitted into the picture with Max Rader.

I had left it at that. Hawk had said not to tell her anything she didn't absolutely have to know.

"It's the way you bolluxed the contact on the steamer," I finally blurted out. "Instead of identifying yourself, you were playing the tart! I don't dig that. And another thing —you've never shown me any identification except a passport that may or may not be yours. I don't understand that either."

She sipped her chocolate with an enigmatic little smile. "I think they are both really very simple, my Nicholas. To take the second of your doubts first—I was not *given* any identification. Nothing to tie me to Bonn, or to AXE. My superior had the thought that if I had been spying on Max Rader for so long, then perhaps he had also been spying on me. Perhaps he *knows* I am the only one who can identify him now! You know what that means?"

"Open and shut," I said. "He'll try to kill you as quick as he can."

A shadow flitted over her lovely face. I noted for the first time that, in certain lights, there was a hint of lavender in the huge gray eyes.

The Baroness replaced her cup in the saucer. She nodded. "But of course. My superior did not want anything found on my body that would lead back to Bonn. Mere routine."

I could accept that. I knew the espionage, and counter-espionage, ropes as well as any man in the world.

"As for playing the tart," she went on, "I did, of course. But I could not be really sure it was you. Your disguise was so excellent. You looked like a dirty sailor. You even smelled. And you had been drinking."

I grinned at her. I was beginning to lose some of my doubts. "All part of the act."

"You played it well, Nicholas. Almost too well. I had only a quick glance at the travel stickers on your suit-case, in the bright lights of the quay at Thonon. I thought they identified you as an AXE agent, but I could not be sure. Then for the rest of the trip you insisted on re-maining in the shadows near the stern. Your face told me nothing, of course. I could not get close enough to read the stickers again without an excuse. I could not declare myself until I was positive. For all I knew, you could be one of Rader's men. So—" Here the Baroness shrugged her shoulders, elegant even in the torn and slightly soiled faille jacket. "So I did the best I could. I became a tart."

I had to admit that it made sense. "And you never got a good chance to read the stickers before I gave you some of old Poindexter's sleeping potion?" I plucked a ball-point pen out of my coat pocket and pointed it at her. "I carry it here, you know. It doesn't write. It squirts."

She did not smile. "At least it does not give one a hangover. No, I had no chance to read the stickers. You were in such a rush, remember. And always in the shad-ows, in the darkest places."

"It pays off," I said grimly. "One does not, as you say, conduct my sort of business in the middle of Times Square at high noon."

She shrugged again. "I suppose not. In any case, I could hardly ask you to stop beneath a street lamp so I could read your suitcase, could I?" The girl smiled at the inanity of the picture.

I admitted that she could not. "But when we got to the Hotel Lux?"

The Baroness pouted her red mouth. "I had no time. I did not want to seem obvious, and you never seemed to get very far away from me. I was beginning to be frightened, to think that I *had* made a mistake and that you—that you would—"

I laughed. "Demand my money's worth?"

"Yes. Then suddenly all the world went black and—and you searched my person! I should hate you for that."

"But you don't?"

"No. You did not harm me. You—you did nothing. I would know. But I would like to have my two little friends back, if you please."

I patted the rhino-hide suitcase beside me. "In there. You'll get them back in due time. Now one more thing, Baroness."

She reached to touch my hand again. "Please, my Nicholas. No more Baroness! Elizabeth, if you will. We are going to be very good friends. I know it."

I had to admit to myself that I knew it too. Hawk's orders or no!

"Okay," I agreed. "Elizabeth it is, if you want it that way. But I'll go on thinking of you as the Baroness, if you don't mind." I gave her a half mocking, half serious smile. "You do *look* like a Baroness, you know."

"I *am* a Baroness," she said, with a touch of her old hauteur. "An old title. My family has been in the *Almanach de Gotha* for—"

"Never mind that now, sweetie. I said there was one more thing—then we've got to cut out of this joint. And that thing is, how did Hondo know where to look this morning? I think I know the answer, but I want to hear your ideas."

She fumbled in her purse and took out the packet of Players I had noticed before, during my search. As I held my lighter for her, she gazed at me steadily through the smoke. "I think my idea is the same as yours, my Nicholas. They were not following you. They were following *me!* They were really Rader's men! They must have followed us from the boat last night."

I studied her through narrowed eyes. My mind was racing. I agreed with her. Not that it made much difference now, except as it might affect my execution of Mission Tiger. She was a danger there. Neither Hawk nor I had counted on this twist. The Baroness was supposed to finger Max Rader for me; but she in turn, by her very presence with me, would finger me for Rader! And I couldn't just hide her someplace until this was over. I needed her with me to identify Max Rader.

"This mess is developing more angles than a spider web," I said crossly. If the Baroness was on the level I had to protect her. That could easily interfere with the mission. But there was no alternative. I *had* to protect her—at least until the mission was completed.

She pointed her cigarette at me. "I know what you are thinking. That I am in the way. Yes?"

I admitted it. "In a way. But I need you. You're the only one who can spot Rader for me."

She regarded me steadily with her huge lavender-gray eyes. "You Americans are not often hypocrites, at least. You are blunt and outspoken. I think I like it."

I tried to ignore that. My thoughts were racing elsewhere. I was feeling more sanguine about Max Rader at the moment. The man would do nothing rash or precipitate. Not after waiting twenty years for a chance at the golden tiger. No. Max Rader would wait and watch and lay his plans carefully. And his plan would be a cunning one, that I could be sure of. Rader had had twenty years to perfect it.

And now that I had thought it over, it was foolish to panic, to worry about Rader obtaining the tiger from the bank of Chardet et Fils. Not unless Hondo was there with him. Neither of them would trust the other! I would have staked my life on that.

I remembered the intensive briefing just before I had left Washington, three days ago. The Brain Boys, the wizards who prepared the briefing and mapped the plans, had come up with several good reasons why Rader and Hondo *had* to trust each other. One of the reasons was probably right. No—I didn't have to worry about Rader grabbing the tiger just yet. There would be a lull now. We were in the eye of the hurricane.

I fumbled in my pocket for the packet of Gauloises. They were the one false note in the façade of Mr. Frank Manning, but in a weak moment I had given all my American cigarettes to the girl in Portofino. Not that it mattered. Mr. Manning was *kaput. Fini.* I, as Nick Carter, could smoke anything I damned well pleased.

I looked at the Baroness. "Okay. I think we'll have to play it this way—they're after you. I'm not blown as yet. Herr Kurz is down the sink at the Hotel Lux. They can't know about Frank Manning, because I got no reaction from those watchers this morning. And Hondo is dead. No sweat there. Anyway, we can assume, at this moment, that Rader and his men are as confused as we are. Probably more so. Hondo's death will raise a little stink, so they won't dare hang around the Hotel Lux too openly. No matter anyway.

"So our problem is—how in hell am I going to keep you with me so you can do your job of spotting Rader, and keep you alive, *and* at the same time keep them from tying me in with you as a possible agent, a danger to them? I can only think of one way we might get away with it. How is your reputation, Baroness—I mean, Elizabeth?"

Her lovely eyes widened. "What on earth are you talking about, Nicholas?"

I smiled my sweetest smile. "Nothing on earth, darling. I'm talking about paradise! A lover's paradise. You and I have got to become lovers, my pet. At least in outward appearance. I'm asking if your reputation is up to it. Would it be in character? This Max Rader is no fool, or so my people tell me, and you say he might know as much about you as you know about him. We couldn't fool him if you've got the reputation of a cast-iron spinster who won't go out without her chastity belt. You beginning to get it?"

The Baroness was pink again. Looking so young again. Too young, I thought. It just couldn't be true. I waited.

Suddenly she laughed. "I think you are in luck, my Nicholas. I have been known to take lovers, yes. I admit it to you—"

"Why not? It's all in the line of business, you know."

She gnawed at a moist lower lip with little white teeth. I thought I detected a hint of mischief in her eyes. Spiked with malice, perhaps?

She nodded. "But of course. Only business, as you say. I think we could play the role of lovers very well. My reputation, as you put it, will live up to it. In character. But you will have to understand that it *is* only business, my Nicholas. A front, as you Americans say." There was definite mischief in her eyes now. Or was it mockery?

"Fine. We'll play it that way, then. We might even get away with it for a time. After all, there *was* the dirty sailor you picked up on the boat last night. Rader's men saw that. They followed us to the Hotel Lux. They must have had their thoughts."

"I'm sure they did."

I realized that the packet of Gauloises I had been fumbling with was empty. "Hell," I muttered.

She pushed the Players toward me. "Have one of these."

I reached into another pocket. "I should have—what's this?"

I put Mr. Shikoku Hondo's false teeth on the table

before us. Until now I had completely forgotten the upper plate I had scooped from the floor in our mad dash from the Hotel Lux.

The Baroness' mouth was a round red O of astonishment. I chuckled. "The late Hondo's teeth. I didn't want to leave them around for the cops."

She made a face. "Ugh! They're horrible. Throw them away!"

But I picked up the false upper plate. I was amused. "Look at this, will you! Buck teeth! They even made them a little buck so they'd match the old ones. Those Japs are sure hell for detail, aren't they?"

"Please, Nicholas! Throw them away. They're making me ill."

I was about to tell her not to be so damned squeamish when suddenly my eyes were riveted on the false teeth. The plate had cracked diagonally. I saw a glint of metal showing through the red neoprene. I tried to fish it out with my fingers. It would not come.

"Nicholas! Really, we should be going. I think I see—"

I held up a commanding hand. "Be quiet!"

I rapped the false teeth gently on the table. The fissure in the neoprene widened. Impatient, I seized the plate in both my hands and tore it apart. A shiny little rod rolled onto the table. I grabbed it. I knew it immediately for what it was. Part of a French key!

My mouth slowly widened in a grin of delight and triumph. The Brain Boys back in Washington had been right after all. They had guessed, or rather they had considered it a possibility, that Max Rader and Shikoku Hondo *each had half of the French key*. Half of the remaining key after it had been wedged into a vault lock and sawn off. No wonder they'd had to trust each other!

And now Hondo's half, like manna from the gods, had literally fallen into my lap.

I laughed out loud. No Swiss bank would accept half of a half key. They were much too circumspect for that. I laughed again. Max Rader, after waiting for nearly twenty years for Hondo to get out of prison so they could claim the golden tiger—Max Rader was now further from the tiger than ever. Hondo was dead and now I had his half of the key. Rader would have to come to me. I could call the shots.

I looked up to find a frowzy waiter at the table. The man had mistaken the rapping on the table for a summons. I shook my head and dropped a handful of francs on the table. I felt generous. I felt marvelous. Ask and it shall be given. Even if you didn't ask, it was sometimes given. I dropped the fragment of French key in my pocket.

I stood up and picked up Gladstone. I winked at the Baroness, slipping easily into my new role. "Come, darling. It's time we were going."

"More than time," she whispered as we approached the door. "There's something I've been trying to tell you. The police—they're just down the way. To the left—they're in another café now."

"Then we'll turn to the right," I said. "And walk slowly, do not run, to the nearest exit. Hand in hand, as lovers should." I turned up my coat collar and pulled the baggy garment around me as we left. It was probably only a routine check, but I would hate to be stopped now. They might be curious about a shirtless man. And if they ever searched Gladstone, the jig was up.

Not now! Not with the French key burning a hole in my pocket! Not with the whole damned game right in my hands!

The Baroness snuggled her hand into mine. She pressed against me, playing her role to the hilt. We're a couple of pretty crummy looking lovers, I thought with wry amusement. But it seemed to be working. There were no shouts. No hands on the shoulder.

Beside me the Baroness said softly: "I think I have it, my Nicholas. A place where we can hide. A very fine place for lovers. It belongs to a very old friend of mine,

but she will not be using it now. I do not even have to
call her for permission. I have the use of the place when-
even I want it. We will even have servants. Shall we go
there?"

I glanced down at her. The top of her honey-amber
head came only to his shoulder. "Where is this paradise?
We can sure use something like that about now."

"About twenty miles up the lake, on the Swiss side.
It will be perfect for us." She slipped her arm through
mine. "For our plan, you know. Playing at being lovers."

"I'm all for it," I said. "But how do we get to this
perfumed garden of romance? Swim?"

"There are launches one can rent. See just ahead?
There is one of the piers now."

"Lead on, sweetheart, and let the play begin."

We headed for the little pier thrusting like a wooden
finger into the calm lake. I risked a backward glance. No
police. No one showing undue interest in us.

The breeze off the lake was brisk and faintly chill.
Flags and bunting flapped bravely around the pier. A
small white launch was moored to the pier, protected
by fenders made of old tires.

As we felt the boards of the pier beneath our feet
the Baroness said: "What was it about the false teeth
that made you so happy, my Nicholas? Has it anything
to do with our business? With the tiger?"

"It has everything to do with it, my cabbage." I bent to
kiss her pretty neck. She pulled away from me, but she
was smiling. "You fool! Not in public. You don't have
to overdo it."

I gazed at her in mock astonishment. "I don't see what
you mean. I thought that was the plan—in public is
exactly where we *do* have to overdo it!"

She frowned. "You know what I mean! But that thing
in the false teeth—?"

"Later," I promised. "Much later."

I began to whistle softly—*Everything's going my way...*

Six

Having completed my usual fifteen minutes stint of strenuous yoga—breathing, head pose, cobra posture, corpse posture (this did not particularly distress me, because I always thought of corpses as being someone else) —having completed these, I did something that was unusual for me. I spent another fifteen minutes in the poses of meditation. First the lotus seat. Then the adept's seat. In this I remained for the balance of the period.

I did two things that my ancient guru, the holy man who had taught me yoga long ago, would not have approved of. I did not close my eyes, and I did not shut out the sounds of the world around me. I had found that yoga worked quite well for me, with these two variations. It was possible to fall *too* deeply into meditation—thus inviting a knife in the back, the odd bullet in the skull, the swift cord of *thuggee!* What odds the manner in which death might come? I had faced the grinning gentleman many times and come off best, and I proposed to go on doing so. Yet ever since I and the Baroness von Stadt had arrived at the Villa Limbo, I had been aware of a growing sense of uneasiness. True, such a feeling was almost second nature to me, an occupational disease as it were. Yet this prescience I was experiencing now was somewhat different. I felt, vaguely, without quite knowing why, that it concerned me personally more than it did Mission Tiger.

Now, as I sat unmoving as a statue in the middle of the large and comfortably furnished room, I realized that the greatest source of my unease was that I did not know *why* I was uneasy. I was certainly in the driver's seat at the moment. I had Hondo's half of the French key, which meant that Max Rader was stymied, behind the eight ball, and so must eventually come out into the open. He would have to play my game, on ground chosen by me. What more could I ask?

The Baroness—Elizabeth—and I had been at Villa Limbo for hours now and, so far as I had been able to determine, it looked like a "safe" house. At least for the time being.

The villa stood on a small, cliffy island two hundred yards off the Swiss shore. There was no phone. The only communication with the shore was by means of a small aluminum skiff moored to the small dock where the launch had deposited us. The oars were in the skiff, but it was chained and padlocked to one of the piles. I had noted this, and many other things, as the Baroness and I climbed the steep, twisting, wooden stairs up the face of the cliff to the villa.

"Your friend must like her privacy," I had commented. The Baroness had been evasive about her friend during the trip from Geneva. Her friend, the Comtesse de Lanquoc, a very old, dear, and valued friend, had once been a famous concert pianist. Now elderly, and suffering badly from arthritis, she lived in seclusion in Paris. Only on rare occasions did she visit the Villa Limbo. Yet she kept it open, kept it staffed, and the Baroness von Stadt was always welcome. Indeed, the Baroness had told me, Villa Limbo was like a second home to her. She came here often and had many possessions here—clothing, books, and similar lares and penates.

Having revealed this much, she had adroitly changed the subject.

Without moving a muscle, I flicked an eye down at my watch. Three minutes to go. Then I would switch on the expensive Telefunken in the corner by the balcony window and see if I could find a newscast from Geneva. I might be able to pick up a shred or two of information about the Hotel Lux and Hondo.

I broke my impassive pose to smile grimly. Max Rader might very likely be doing the same thing.

I was conscious of a womanly presence at the crack of the door for a full minute before I spoke. I could smell her, a vivid perfume that spoke of many things, but not danger, and at last I said: "Come on in, Mignonne! No fair peeking! What is it you want?"

I had met the permanent staff briefly on arrival. It consisted only of a maid, Mignonne Franchette, and an enormously fat man of all work whom the Baroness had addressed simply as Osman.

Mignonne Franchette swished into the room now, rustling and perfumey and not at all abashed. "If M'sieur does not wish to be spied on," she said boldly, "he should not sit around in his underwear." After showering, I had donned a pair of white boxer shorts. They were of Irish linen, tailored, and had cost me a fortune.

There was a boldness in the maid's eyes as she halted only a step or two from me and looked me up and down. Boldness, and something more. Something I had seen in the eyes of so many women. It had little to do with love, though some women described it as such.

Desire. Naked lust.

I was used to rolling with the passes. I grinned at her. "I'm decent," I said. At the puzzlement on her broad, pretty, peasant face I added, "An old show-business expression, Mignonne. Skip it. What do you want?"

The maid did not meet my look. She had sleek black hair, dark as obsidian, pulled back severely from her temples and caught in a shiny chignon. Her widely spaced eyes matched her hair—glittering jet. They did not meet mine now, but continued to rove over my body, crawling over my flesh like little black mice.

I began to feel uncomfortable. Enough was enough.

"Mignonne. What is it? Did you come here simply to admire my physique?" As a line, I knew, it wasn't much. In fact, the whole little tableau was beginning to remind me of an old French farce, badly done. The girl, stockily well built in her crisp black uniform and white apron, her tiny wisp of a white cap, lent credence to the illusion.

With reluctance, Mignonne raised her glance. Her dark eyes met mine. Wells of purest invitation.

"It is the Baroness," she said. "She wishes to know if you will join her for a swim before dinner?" She looked past me now, over my shoulder at the iron balcony and the sun-sparkled lake beyond. Her tones were again those of the servant.

"Tell her I'll be glad to," I said. "But where? Isn't the lake a little cold this time of year?" Not for me, of course. They immersed you in a tank of ice water at Purg. But for a woman? Especially one who had had a pretty rough night and day so far?

"There is a conservatory, M'sieur. A heated pool. The Baroness is there now. If M'sieur wishes, I will show him the way, *non?*" Boldness flashed in her dark eyes again. She came a step closer. She seemed to be struggling with an overwhelming desire to reach out and touch me.

"No," I said crisply. She *wasn't* a bad-looking kid. A little solid, perhaps, but with every inch of it in the right place. Being offered to me on a silver platter. I chuckled. At least Hawk couldn't squawk about it. Mignonne *wasn't* working with me.

The girl had caught the chuckle. "M'sieur is amused?"

"Yes and no," I said. "Beat it, now. Tell the Baroness I'll be there in ten minutes."

"Beat it, M'sieur?" Her rather large teeth, sparkling white, glowed behind full, red lips. She moved closer. "You wish to beat me?" Mignonne appeared to think it was a first-class idea.

I retreated. "No, for Pete's sake. Go—scram! Get out!"

I pointed to the door. My French was more than adequate, but American slang was a different matter.

But Mignonne did not immediately go. Instead, she put out a hand and squeezed my bicep. Her fingertips caressed it almost in awe. "You have the big muscles, M'sieur. Most amazing. *Formidable!*"

I laughed. Taking her by the arm, I guided her firmly to the door. "You are a nice girl, Mignonne, and I love you—at least I admire your lack of inhibition—but go! Tell the Baroness ten minutes. I will find the conservatory by myself."

At the door she turned, her full, firm breasts suddenly pressed against my naked chest. The smell of her perfume and flesh was overpowering. Mignonne flicked a finger at my newly shaven chin. "It is very lonely here," she said in a teasing voice. "Alone on this place with only that horrible fat one for company. Perhaps, M'sieur, you will find time to be kind to Mignonne? I am very good in bed! And the Baroness would never suspect. I am most discreet."

"I'll just bet you are," I said. "Out, girl!" I gave her a little push into the corridor. Mignonne gave me a final smile and sauntered away, hips swaying, buttocks quivering.

I closed the door and locked it. Whew! Wow! Maybe the Villa Limbo wasn't such a safe house after all! I leered at myself in a tall cheval glass standing in a corner —this had been a woman's room at one time—and went out onto the small sleeping porch that served as a bedroom for the suite.

Gladstone lay open on the bed. I began to rummage through it. I had a little problem. In fact, I had several little problems. Clothes, for one. I was almost out of clean clothes. A sport shirt, slacks, a modest hound's-tooth jacket, socks, and tan loafers. That was all. They would do well enough for now. Later—if there was any later—I could reequip myself at the *dépôt* in Geneva.

The immediate problem was the fragment of French key. I took it from the elastic waistband of my boxer trunks and studied it. I held it to my lips and kissed it with a flourish. I wasn't going to be parted from it. Not yet. I certainly couldn't leave it around in the suite while the Baroness and I swam, and ate, and—and did whatever we might do.

So where in the hell to hide it? I was going to have to swim in my underwear trunks, and they had no pockets. Remind old Poindexter, I thought. Every agent's kit to be complete with swimming trunks from now on.

As I puzzled over the problem, I took my three most faithful friends out of the suitcase and checked them over. Everything was in first-class order.

I would have to leave Wilhelmina behind. You could hardly walk around with a Luger tucked into your shorts. Might cause comment. And Pierre? Well, Pierre could go along in the pocket of my terry-cloth robe.

Hugo? I thrust the nasty little stiletto into the elastic of my trunks. Not too bad, at that. The Baroness might wonder. So let her. She was on my side. Wasn't she? Anyway, I never went anywhere without at least one of my pals. In my profession there was one axiom it didn't pay to ignore: Never be caught without a weapon.

The question of what to do with the French key remained. I was loath even to trust it to Gladstone. Too important. Gladstone was very nearly burglarproof, to be sure—if you opened him incorrectly a hidden mechanism triggered a stream of tear gas into the burglar's face, and there was a very small alarm bell that made one hell of a noise! Gladstone was almost impregnable. But for the French key, almost wasn't good enough.

I sighed. I knew what I was going to have to do. Nothing else for it. Damn it! The things an AXE agent had to do were not always so dignified.

From the suitcase I took a small rubber sheath, like a fingerstall, and a little tube of petroleum jelly. I went into the bathroom. I might be a little uncomfortable, but the French key would be safe.

As I left the suite and locked the door, I was conscious of growing excitement. I knew it did not altogether have to do with Mission Tiger. I'm always honest with myself, so I had no trouble recognizing the symptoms. The weird encounter with Mignonne Franchette had aroused me.

I believe that this was, except for Mignonne, a safe house. For the moment. The Baroness von Stadt was lovely, by her own admission a woman who took lovers, and she was obviously attracted to me. Under all the banter, the chaffing about playing at being lovers, I had sensed the truth. I did not think she would refuse me. So why not make the most of each shining hour? Even if I didn't exactly trust her yet. Now was now. Later was later. And a young and beautiful woman is always—just that!

The Villa Limbo was a great, rambling place of white and pink stucco. It boasted a roof of red tile and exquisite wrought iron balconies. It crowned the steep-sided little island like the villa of some ancient Roman prince. The island was small and dense with shrubbery and trees. A great many conifers mingled with thick stands of larch, birch, and oak. On my way to the house that day, I had noted a number of paths leading away from it, presumably to every part of the island, radiating from the villa like spokes from a hub.

I might, I thought as I went down a broad iron-bannistered stair to the ground floor, explore a bit. In the morning, perhaps. I could not abide inaction, even in bed, and exploring would be something to do until Max Rader found me. Or I found Max.

In the meantime, there was the Baroness. Elizabeth!

I had positioned the conservatory, or greenhouse, as the girl and I had entered the villa earlier. I made my way there now, leaving the main house through a postern and walking along a wide graveled path hedged on both sides by yew. It was a curving path, and as I rounded the last curve before reaching the conservatory, I encountered the fat man of all work. The one the Baroness had called Osman.

I had never seen anything quite like Osman before. I remembered that as a child I had seen advertisements for tires that consisted of a man *made* of tires. A very fat man made of very fat tires. Osman reminded me of that ad.

Osman's tires were made of blubber. From his neck to his ankles he was encased in little wrinkles and ripples of darkish blubber. I guessed that he was probably Syrian, or a Turk. The grotesque thing was that he dressed like a Swiss mountaineer. When I first saw him, I had found it hard not to laugh.

Now, as I rounded the curve in the path and saw Osman sitting on a stone bench smoking a pipe, the urge to laugh returned. The *lederhosen,* the frilled and gaily colored shirt, the yoke, and the little green hat with its feather were almost too much!

Osman looked up and saw me approaching. He stood up immediately, amazingly quick and agile for a man who must top four hundred pounds. I noted that fact mentally. Not such a slob as he looks.

"Good afternoon, sir," said Osman. "A fine day, sir." His manner exceeded the ordinary obsequiousness of the European servant. He was nearly groveling, as though on command, he would fall to the ground and start kissing your feet. And his voice. High, shrill, lilting, well up into the treble range. It grated on my nerves, coming as it did from such a huge mass of lard.

I gave Osman a courteous "Good afternoon." The man stood there, hat in hand, obviously nervous, staring back at me. He was totally bald, and had small, piggy eyes encased in rolls of fat. I experienced a genuine pang of sympathy for Mignonne Franchette. It *couldn't* be much fun to be alone on an island with this specimen!

I suddenly became aware that Osman, though subservient and correct, was examining me very closely. He did not stare, he kept his little eyes downcast, but he was missing nothing. I could not mistake the sensation of being closely appraised—I was too familiar with it. So Osman was curious. So what? He was probably as lonely and frustrated—certainly frustrated!—as Mignonne. Curious, too. The Villa Limbo did not get many visitors these days, according to the Baroness.

"Is the Baroness in the greenhouse?"

"Oh, yes! Yes, sir! She has been waiting for you, sir." Osman would have bowed if his fat had permitted it. He swept his ridiculous green hat in the direction of the glass house. His voice soared into the high scales. "She has been waiting for some time, sir."

I smiled at him. I did not like anything about the man. Not too unusual for me, because, actually, I did not like many people. I knew them too well. But Osman revolted me for some reason I could not at the moment recognize, and I was afraid I would show it. I had not the slightest objection to killing anyone who deserved it, but I did not like to hurt feelings wantonly.

As I went on, I could feel Osman watching me. I pitied him. Poor slob! Four hundred odd pounds of blubber. What must go on in his mind? He could never get close to a woman, not even physically!

I pushed open a tall glass door and entered a steamy jungle atmosphere. The light robe I had on, with Pierre nestling snugly in the pocket, was suddenly too much. I took it off and draped it over one arm. For a moment I stood there, just looking around. The Comtesse de Lanquoc, I thought, must have exotic tastes. And she would have to be loaded to afford a place like this.

It was like stepping into a jungle or a rain forest. Dense verdure everywhere, comprising every shade of green, relieved by the brilliance of tropical flowers. Huge waxen-winged butterflies, as large as bats, fluttered.

Pastel birds darted like shining arrows from tree and bush.

I saw the leopard staring cruelly down from a tree limb. Instinctively, I reached for Hugo. Then I laughed. The leopard was stuffed! Stuffed, but damned realistic.

Several paths led from the door into the jungle. As I hesitated a moment, trying to decide which one to take, I heard voices. A voice. A radio. I smiled. The Baroness must be listening to the news. Something I had intended to do, but Mignonne had interrupted. I set off down the path, following the announcer's metallic tones.

The path led to a little clearing in the make-believe jungle. So realistic was the camouflage, so artfully done, that I couldn't shake the sensation of actually being in the jungle.

The Baroness von Stadt was splashing about in the pool. She was nude. I watched in appreciation as she swam aimlessly to and fro, then lifted her taut white buttocks to dive from the surface. She came up blowing, the honey-colored hair a silky wet mask over her features, water cascading from her superb breasts. She did not see me watching, and dove again.

Near the pool were several inflated rubber mats. On one of them was a white robe and two tiny bits of golden bikini. Nearby was a silver ice bucket with a bottle cooling in it. Near this was a large wicker lunch hamper. On another rubber mat the radio, a small transistor, was still talking to itself.

The Baroness came up again, blowing, like a sprite rising from the foam. Ondine, I thought, as I stepped from my hiding place. A sea witch! I would have to be careful. I meant to be. I also meant to have her.

I went to the pool's edge. "Me Tarzan," I grinned. "You Jane?"

"Nicholas!" She swam to me, her red mouth smiling, making no effort to conceal her body. "Where have you been, my Nicholas? I sent Mignonne hours ago."

"You mean fifteen minutes ago, baby. Never mind—

you feeling better now? You're looking tremendous." I gave her a mock leer.

The Baroness crossed her arms over her breasts. "Don't stare. I am not ashamed of my body. Nor am I ashamed of what I do with it! And in answer to your question—I feel wonderful. I am in—how do you Americans say?— I am in the pink. I had a bath and a nap."

I knelt by the side of the pool and considered her dripping phocine pelt. Sleek and pretty as a seal pup.

"You certainly are in the pink," I admitted. "Every beautiful inch of you."

Laughing, the Baroness clung to the edge of the pool. She uncovered her breasts and went about the business of combing her soaking hair with her fingers. I looked at her with frank appreciation. I have always considered myself something of a connoisseur of breasts, and hers were per-fection. Perfect pears, perfectly placed on her rib cage, a just-right size of mammarial firmness, with tiny blue veins lacing the cream. Each tipped with a glowing little rose-bud.

Eminently kissable, I thought. Kissable in the extreme. Made for kissing. And hadn't it been Herrick who had written, "Gather ye rosebuds while ye may"? In my pro-fession, that was an axiom to live by. While you did live.

Yet some imp prompted me to risk spoiling the mood by saying, "I'm glad to see you don't swim in it, at least."

The Baroness flicked her eyes up at me. In the green light her eyes were again a lavender-gray, shot with golden sparks. She halted in the act of brushing wet hair back from her high, pale forehead.

"I don't swim in what, my Nicholas?"

"The locket."

A half smile had been quivering on her lips. Now it vanished. She looked away. "I—I had nearly forgotten that you searched me while I slept. Of course you would know about the locket and—and the picture. But do you have to speak of it now? At this time?"

"I'm sorry," I said. I was.

Her smile returned. "Then I forgive you. Now come in and swim with me. Later there is wine. And I had Mignonne prepare some food." She pointed to the hamper and the silver cooling bucket. "But first we will swim together, yes?"

I hesitated. With cold eyes, I examined the pseudo-jungle around us. The bright-colored birds darted and twittered. The transistor radio droned on, now in French, now in German. I rolled my robe into a tight bundle and placed it at the edge of the pool. Pierre should be safe there for a time. I reached down to brush my fingers against the cold metal of Hugo, snug in the waistband of my trunks.

I took another long, lingering look around. My instinct told me it was safe. For now. *I* was safe. And even KILLMASTER had to relax once in a while.

The Baroness von Stadt encircled my ankle with firm, wet fingers. She stared up at me, her eyes filled with a strange and misty invitation. Very softly, she said: "Even here you are cautious. Even here, just before we make love, you are afraid. It is bad, terrible, that you must always live so, my darling!"

I reached down to stroke the wet amber hair. I was glad that she had declared herself. The frank admission of intent, the affectionate term, these cleared the air. No more fencing between us. Later, when it was over—well, that was later.

"Yes," I admitted, "It's a lousy way to live. But it's my life. But you're right—we shouldn't talk or think about things like that now. This is our time—just the two of us."

With one of her mercurial changes of mood, the Baroness laughed. She tugged at my ankle, trying to drag me off balance. "You think so, my Nicholas! You think so! But you must catch me first." For just a moment, in that little jungle glade filled with greenish twilight, she sounded like a schoolgirl.

"I'll catch you," I promised. I went after her in a long, swooping dive. I caught her in three strokes. She turned, laughing and fighting, a squirming white nymph in my arms.

"You mustn't struggle so," I whispered. "Someone might be watching. Remember, we're pretending to be lovers." I pulled her close to me. I was standing now, the water up to my chest. I felt the soft, firm coolness of her breasts as they brushed my flesh. Her nipples were rigid.

The Baroness von Stadt ceased all pretense. Unsmiling, she came into my arms. She pressed her lips against mine, her mouth open, her tongue grasping for mine.

For a long time we kissed, our mouths glued together, our tongues entwined like two red snakes.

Finally the Baroness gasped, "I do not pretend now, Nicky! Oh, I do not pretend now! I want you. I want you!" She wrapped her long white legs about me, squeezing my waist in a scissor hold. But when I tried gently to break the hold, she resisted and whispered, "No! Not here. Carry me out, my darling. Carry me. The rubber mat . . ."

Seven

There was little preliminary play, no tender teasing, no slow arousing. The Baroness did not want it that way. She was avid, demanding. As I carried her to the rubber mat, her hands were questing, seeking, toying with my body.

I placed her gently on the mat and knelt beside her. But the Baroness twisted up, her mouth seeking mine. A lovely, white-skinned succubus, leeching at my flesh, my soul, it seemed. She fought when I pushed her away. She did not want to stop what she was doing.

I forced her down on the mat. "No," I said harshly. "What are you trying to do, drive me crazy?"

"I am already crazy," she moaned. "Crazy for you, Nicky." She lay beneath me, gasping and panting, moving her head slowly from side to side. "Hurry then, hurry . . ."

Within a very few moments, I knew that I had very nearly met my match at lovemaking. This lovely creature, now sobbing and crying and entwining herself about me, was demanding and insatiable. I sensed that she had not had an adequate lover for a long time. I smiled a little grimly as I sought to adjust my rhythm to hers. The Baroness had never encountered a Nick Carter before. How could she? There was only one!

Nevertheless, as the frenzied lovemaking continued, as the pace stepped up and the tempo increased, I realized that I was being tested as never before. It was going to be a near thing! My rigorously trained body, my perfect condition, the hours of breathing exercises and yoga, all would be called into play before I subdued, dominated, and satisfied this willing, frantic creature beneath me.

But dominate her I would. Satisfy her I would. I was determined to take her to a peak she had never climbed before.

Elizabeth von Stadt seemed to sense my intent and determination. There was no speech between us now. Only animal sounds. She sighed and moaned and gasped and uttered little Germanic obscenities that I was sure she had never learned in the family manor. Her long white legs were rubber things, tentacles, flailing and threshing, releasing and grasping. She thrust her taut breasts at me, demanding kisses, then took them away only to thrust them back again.

At times I became deliberately brutal, not because I wanted to hurt her, but because I was determined to possess her to the core, to the innermost depths of her body. The Baroness welcomed me with frantic lunges of her own. She came up to meet the onslaught with a fierceness that matched my own. She was an insatiable red gaping maw that must be somehow filled, somehow tamed.

As we both rushed toward the precipice, toward the long tumble into scarlet languor, she relaxed a bit and let me set the pace. She clung to me, she wrapped herself in me, as though every cubic inch of her velvety hide must touch every inch of mine.

I fell back on an old device that had stood me in good stead many times. I managed to retain one small cool spot in my brain. From this vantage point, with the tiny part of myself that remained aloof, uncommitted, I watched the Baroness.

I had watched it happen so often. A sad, lovely, and terrible sight. A beautiful woman coming apart. Caught up by passion, locked in the toils of desire, striving fiercely for release. All glamor and dignity were gone. The façade, the mask, the face the world usually saw was obliterated. Money no longer existed, nor did clothes, position in life, status—there was nothing but a raw desire. At times like this, woman, any woman, lost control. Her facial muscles went flaccid, her eyes rolled back in her head, she became a thing of malleable flesh, to be shaped and rolled and manipulated and deliciously tortured.

The Baroness was fast approaching such a state. Her head lolled back, the cords in her long white throat standing out. Her eyes were closed, her red mouth wide open, and she kept crying out: *"Quel homme! quel homme!"* What a man! What a man!

She switched to soft German, the words burbling huskily in her throat. *"Liebchen! Liebchen!"*

We were very near it now. Her cries wandered off into faintly accented English. "Nicky—please—just there—Nicky—no—yes—Nicky—Nicky—Nicky . . ."

She screamed as though I had driven a dagger into her heart.

At the same moment, my own world exploded in a pink mushrooming cloud. I seized her fiercely and we clung together, digging our claws into the rough hide of the world as it tried to spin us off into space. Then the long, gentle slide into darkness and peace.

I knew the danger. I had always known it, always fought against it. The soft chains of lassitude could be as dangerous as a viper. Death did not always present an iron face; sometimes it came wrapped in a guise of peace and fulfillment. It was a treacherous time.

I recovered first. In a few minutes I was once again alert, my senses attuned once more to the real world, the dangerous world around me.

The muttering radio gradually penetrated my temporarily beguiled brain. Neither of us had thought to turn it off, nor cared, and it had maundered on during our lovemaking.

The announcer was speaking in French now: "Police are puzzled by the strange affair at the Hotel Lux—"

I sat bolt upright. Beside me the Baroness lay breathing quietly. "What is it, Nicky?"

"Quiet!"

The announcer was going on: "Police are requesting that Herr Rubli Kurz, of Zurich, get in touch with them at once. It is believed that Herr Kurz, who registered early this morning at the Hotel Lux with a woman, may be able to throw some light on this strange affair . . ."

I smiled down at the Baroness. "They'll wait a long time for Herr Kurz to show. Wonder why they don't mention Hondo's body. Maybe they did and I missed it."

She held up a hand. "Shhh—he's talking again."

A commercial over, the announcer resumed. "According to Georges Bezant, the concierge at the Hotel Lux, the masked men appeared to be searching for something. They tore apart the room occupied by Herr Kurz and conducted an intensive search of the back court. Monsieur Bezant says all the men wore stocking masks. He was held at gun point, but was not harmed. When the men left, he immediately summoned the police, who had already paid one visit to the Hotel Lux in the affair of Herr Rubli Kurz. There are certain other puzzling features about 'l'affaire Lux' as the police are beginning to call it. We will keep our audience posted as matters develop. And now—"

The man went into a commercial for Pernod. I switched off the radio, a new worm of unease crawling in me. What about Hondo? No mention of his body. Nothing.

I didn't like it. Three alternatives raced through my mind. Hondo was dead, the police had found him and were keeping quiet; Hondo was dead, but his bully boys, the watchers, had managed to get his body away; Hondo was not dead!

I had made a mistake and I knew it. I had *assumed*

something without concrete evidence. And yet—how could a frail character like Hondo survive that terrible kick in the groin, plus a long fall to a concrete court? Usually when KILLMASTER killed them they stayed dead! But this *could* be the odd chance, the one in a million . . .

Elizabeth von Stadt was waiting quietly for me to admit her to my thoughts. Her long fingers were stroking my flank tenderly. Her eyes were closed. Without opening them, she said, "It is business again, yes? Even now! Even here in this paradise. I hate the world sometimes. Oh, how I *hate* it!"

I regarded her in the greenish light that was thickening now as the day ended outside the glass house. The birds were quieting down. I was surprised at the tenderness in my voice. "I know, baby. Elizabeth. But no use cursing the way things are. We've always got to come back to it —face life. Or death."

"Why?"

I grinned and stroked her cheek. "Stop talking like a woman. Snap out of it for now. As my boss and foster-pater always says, business before pleasure." At the moment, I had to confess, it was the other way round. But Hawk wouldn't have to know that.

Hawk! I would have to contact him first thing in the morning. Getting to the *dépôt* in Geneva and back might be something of a problem, but I would find a way.

"You are now working for AXE again," I told the Baroness. "An operative temporarily assigned to me. So get with it, von Stadt! Shape up or ship out!"

She sighed and made a little face. She stretched luxuriously. "I love you when you bully me, *liebchen*." She frowned. "No, I do *not* love you. I have never really loved any man, I think. But, oh my *liebchen*, I have such a tender lust for you!"

She reached for me, but I pushed her hand away. "I

know—you love me, but your heart belongs to Daddy, eh?"

For a moment she stopped breathing. I felt her smooth body go tense all over. Her eyelids quivered, but she kept them closed. In a faint, cold voice she asked, "Why did you say that, Nicky?"

I said I didn't exactly know why, and that was the truth. It had simply been one of those fairly inane, off the cuff remarks that everyone makes from time to time. But it had sure as hell gotten a reaction out of the Baroness.

A second later she brushed it off. She put her hand on my leg and squeezed it. "I am sorry, Nicky. I did not mean to snap at you. But that word—Daddy. I used to call him that, you know. Never Father. Always Daddy."

"I'm sorry too, honey," I said. "I didn't think. Let's forget it, shall we, and get back to this thing? We *do* have to go to work, you know. Okay?"

"Okay." The Baroness relaxed and put her hands beneath her head. Her breasts, no longer urgent now, rested on her rib cage in shimmering, milk-white globes. "We can work here, no? It will be so pleasant. To work just like this. Yes, Nicky? There is nothing to do, nowhere to go tonight. That is so?"

I repressed an urge to kiss her flat belly. I was puzzled at my own thoughts, my own behavior. Somehow, incredibly, the Baroness von Stadt was affecting me differently from any other of the hundreds of women I had known.

"That is so," I told her finally. "Our work is going to be mostly talk—meaning that I'm going to ask questions and you are going to answer them. First I want to know more about this place. And about your friend, the Comtesse de Lanquoc. I think we're in a safe house, for now, but I've got to *know*. I don't like to work in the dark."

"The time has come," the Baroness murmured sleepily, "to speak of many things . . ."

I gave her a little punch just beneath her left breast. Not enough to hurt, but enough to convince her I meant business. The time for fun and games was over.

"Wake up and snap to," I said harshly. "I mean it. Now about the two people here—Mignonne and Osman. What do you know about them? They permanent? Been here a long time?"

The Baroness rubbed her side and gave me a reproachful look. "You needn't be so rough, darling! Well, Mignonne is new. This is the first time I have ever seen her. The Comtesse's regular maid, Annette, is with her in Paris. In the last letter I had from the Comtesse, some time ago, she mentioned hiring Mignonne."

"And Osman? The fat man? He seems an odd sort of creep to find around a place like this."

"Perhaps odd, yes. For most people. But he has been here for ages. He is much older than he looks. He was here the—the first time I ever came to the Villa Limbo."

There was an odd hesitancy in her voice, and she did not look at me. In the fast-dropping green twilight, she was only a white blur beside me. I decided to pursue the point. There *was* something here. Perhaps germane to my business, perhaps not, but I had better know.

"I think you're holding back something about the Comtesse and about Osman," I said. "I know you are. I think you'd better tell me."

There was a long pause before she answered. "I had rather not, Nicky. It does not concern us, believe me. It has nothing to do with Max Rader or with our mission. I promise you that."

"I'll be the judge of that. Tell me about it." I paused. "That's an order, Baroness!"

Her sigh was long. "Very well. I—I met the Comtesse a long time ago, when I was very young. Not yet twenty. She liked me, and I, after I became accustomed to her strangeness, I liked her. She was very kind to me, and I needed kindness. I have not found much of it in my life."

"How was she strange?"

Again the long silence. Then: "She—does not like men. She likes women."

"Don't beat around the bush with me. You mean she's a lesbian?"

"Yes."

"And she took you under her wing? You lived with her here at the villa?"

The Baroness stirred in the gloom. A match flared as she lit a cigarette. In the brief saffron light her eyes regarded me steadily.

"Yes. We did live here at the villa. For a very short time. Then I left. I—I am not so inclined myself. Surely you know that, Nicky. After what we have just done together."

"You don't have to justify yourself to me," I told her. "I don't give a damn about your sex life. I'm only trying to see all the angles in this thing."

"There are no angles, Nicky. Not here at the villa. The Comtesse and I parted friends. I have free run of the place, as you see, and I have many things here. I visit occasionally. And this morning, when we were running, I thought of this place. It is good that we had it to come to, I think. If not, perhaps Rader or the police would have had us by now." Her tone was a little tart.

"Okay," I assented. "I'll buy that. Or most of it. But I still don't quite dig Osman. Somehow he sticks in my craw."

I was a little surprised to hear her chuckle. "I think I know why. You are not the first real man—and what a man you are, my Nicky—to react to Osman like this. You just don't understand about him—he's a eunuch."

So that was it! That explained the shrill voice, the obesity, the groveling manner. I had seen castrates before, but that had been long ago, on a mission in Africa, and they had all been young boys. I had never expected to find a full-grown eunuch on an island in Lac Léman.

"I suppose it makes sense," I acknowledged, "in a weird sort of way. And knowing about the Comtesse."

"It always made sense to her," said the Baroness. "She cannot abide the sight or presence of men. Osman is no man, so he makes the perfect servant and caretaker. For the Comtesse!"

I lit a cigarette. "About the Comtesse again—is there any chance at all—even the barest possible chance—that she could be tied in with Max Rader? Or even with Hondo? Is there a possibility that Rader could know about this place?"

The Baroness laughed throatily. "Impossible—at least the first is impossible. The Comtesse has never had anything to do with politics or violence, and she would not even spit on a person like Max Rader. She has always lived very much aloof from the world, Nicky. You would have to know her to really understand. Her whole life has been spent with and for her music. She was a great pianist, you understand. And now she is just a lonely old lady with arthritic hands, living in Paris and remembering the past. She is in her late sixties now. She was in her middle fifties when she—when I—met her."

I remembered my thoughts as I'd gazed at the sleeping girl in the Hotel Lux that morning. At first glance she had seemed young—very young. Then not quite so young, when you studied the fine lines in the beautiful face. I remembered thinking that the lines indicated experience and suffering. It appeared that I had been right about the experience bit, at least. This kid *had* been around!

Now I admitted to satisfaction about the Comtesse. "But do you think Max Rader could have spotted this place? Is it possible? He must have quite an organization. Those men who raided the Hotel Lux this afternoon were his. Must have been. Hondo couldn't have an organization like that, not in Geneva. Those were Rader's men, and they were looking for Hondo's false teeth."

That last sentence brought a recurring itch to my mind that I did not like. Not at all. Because if Rader's men were looking for Shikoku Hondo's false teeth, that could only mean that Hondo had *told* Rader where he was concealing his half of the French key. And that didn't make sense. Hondo would not trust Max Rader, any more than Rader would trust Hondo. I could not imagine Hondo producing his half of the key until he and Rader were actually at the bank. Not after Hondo had taken every precaution to guard himself! No—something was way out of kilter. Something was wrong with the way the whole picture was developing. But I put it aside for the time being.

"I suppose Max Rader *could* know about this island, the villa," the girl was saying. "I don't see *how,* though. But anything is *possible*. Especially in this crazy business."

I leaned over to kiss her lips, very lightly. "Okay. We'll forget that for now. Even if Rader knows we're here, he can't do much at the moment. He's in a bind and he knows it. I've got something he needs, that he must have, and he won't take any chances on anything happening to me until he's ready for it to happen. Meaning it must happen under circumstances controlled by him. So he can get what he wants before I die."

The Baroness reached to touch me. "Don't, Nicky! Please don't talk like that!"

I settled beside her on the rubber mat. It was completely dark now in the conservatory and outside. It would be faintly chill out in the September night, but in the glass house, amid the exotic flowers and trees and the sleeping birds, the stuffed carnivores, there was the caressing warmth of a tropical night. The perfume of the girl's body, satiated for the time being, seeped into my nostrils. It had been a most gratifying experience, one I would never forget.

"There's a lot I want to know about you and Max Rader and your work with Bonn," I said. "Things I must know. Things I would already know if we hadn't gotten off on the wrong foot this morning."

"You shouldn't have doped me," she whispered. Her lips slid over my cheek.

"Nobody's perfect," I said.

I asked her the question I had asked Hawk over the scrambler that morning. "How come *you're* the only one who knows what Rader looks like now, after his plastic surgery? How do you know he even *had* plastic surgery?"

"Perhaps," the Baroness von Stadt said, "I had better start at the beginning. I will be brief. In Bonn they have taught me how to make reports—to be succinct. First, then, I was born—"

"Cut the clowning."

"I do not clown, Nicky. I will tell you a little of myself along with the rest. It will help you to understand many things about me. *Why* I work for Bonn, for one thing, when I hate it. And when you understand, perhaps you will trust me a little more. As you do not do now."

"I trust you all right," I said. "It's just that I'm the most careful guy in the entire world. Go on."

"All right. I was born. My father was the Graf von Stadt, a very old title in East Prussia. My mother was English—they met when Papa was attached to the German Embassy in London . . ."

"Elizabeth? That's where it came from? I thought it was English."

"Yes. My English grandmother's name. But that is not important. I am being to the point, remember?"

"Sorry."

"They hanged my father—you saw the picture in my locket. They made me watch it."

Even I could feel sick at my guts, and I did now. "I didn't think even the Nazis could stoop that low!"

"There is nothing to which they did not stoop. I had to watch them hang Pa—my father. I was ten years old. My mother was dead, but they came for me and took me to the execution. It was to be a lesson—it was to teach me what happened to enemies of the Reich. Do I have to tell you who it was that came to get me, who took me to the execution, then took me back to my aunt's afterward?"

"Max Rader?"

"Indeed. He was very close to Hitler then. Do you wonder that I have never forgotten or forgiven? I have nightmares still—seeing my father in agony, dangling on the wire, strangling to death. I would like, Nicky, if it can be arranged, to kill Rader myself."

Her words, her tone sent a little chill racing down my spine. That lovely flesh was only a layer over steel and ice.

"I can't promise that," I said. "I usually do the killing when it's required. Go on."

"The next part I do not like to even think about. When the war ended, I had no one but my old aunt. She died soon after I entered my teens. Until that time we had gotten by—not too badly, because American officers were billeted in my aunt's house. They were kind to us. Some of them"—the Baroness gave a bitter little laugh—"some of them tried to be *too* kind to me. I did not mind particularly. I was not an ordinary teen-aged girl, though I looked like one. I grew up in one minute—the time it took my father to die on that wire. So when my aunt died and the authorities were going to put me in an institution, I ran away."

"But surely there was someone," I said. "Friends of your father, your mother's people in England, relatives in East Prussia?"

"There was no one!" Her cigarette glowed in the dark beside me. I thought of the ruby eyes of the tiger I was after. That Max Rader was after. A jackal, that one. A jackal after a tiger.

"How did you live?" I knew the answer, but I wanted to keep her talking. Still trying to catch her in one lie. So far she seemed to be genuine.

The Baroness' velvety skin was against my own, and I felt her shrug. "How *does* one live in a conquered city? I did as all the others did. I worked at what I could—I was in the black market, I worked in cabarets. I—I—sold things." Her voice broke. "Including myself!"

Suddenly she rolled over and came into my arms. "Nicky, oh, Nicky! If you know how many men I have had! Just to be able to eat!" She began to weep softly. I held her and kissed her cheek and felt the salt of her tears. For the first time in my life, I felt inadequate.

After a moment or two she pulled away. "I'm sorry. I am a fool. Let me get on, then. I survived. Even a Baroness must eat. I *did* eat. And I never forgot Max Rader!"

"I'll bet you didn't," I said softly. "Tell me about that sonofabitch. How did he miss getting hanged after the war?"

"Incredible luck. The Devil does take care of his own, I think. Rader was tried for war crimes—and acquitted."

"Hard to believe."

"I know. I could not believe it at first. One of the witnesses lied, perjured himself, and Rader got off. But that did not mean he was forgotten—not by me or by the West German intelligence police. They are very good, you know. Really good. They are built around a core of the old Abwehr."

"I know about them." I had been thoroughly briefed on the relatively new, but excellent, West German intelligence.

The Baroness sighed. "I was furious when Rader got off. I had certain connections, and eventually I came to work with intelligence. I was a part-timer, you understand. I had other jobs. But my work with intelligence helped me keep an eye on Max Rader. It was not a constant watch. I could not do that, and anyway it would have been a waste of time. He was lying very low. Being very much the good reformed German."

I chuckled. "Keeping his nose clean."

"I do not understand that, but no matter. Rader settled in Hamburg. He had a little job there, a little house in the suburbs. For years he did nothing. Now and then I would go to Hamburg to check on him. I would watch the house, observe his comings and goings. I was sure that one day I would catch him in something for which he could be punished. Even executed."

"That was wrong," I told her. "Bad tradecraft, as my boss would say. Sooner or later a watched animal will know that it is being watched. Especially if the same person does the watching, in the same place, all the time. It has to be broken up."

"Perhaps. I am really just an amateur. Anyway, I was doing this on my own time, you understand. My people were not forgetting Rader, but there was nothing against him at the time. They are professionals. Everything is business with them. To me it was personal—I hated! How I hated!"

"I can believe that," I murmured. "I saw the locket, remember?"

"Yes. So you understand. Well, at last my spying was successful. About six months ago I was in Hamburg. As usual, I checked on Max Rader. He was gone. He had sold his house and disappeared. I was surprised and angry. I checked every way I could, but I found nothing. It was as though Max Rader had disappeared into thin air. At just the wrong time—the witness who cleared him at his trial was near death, and had decided to tell the truth. Also, it was clear that the statute of limitations would not go into effect as had been planned. It would be extended. I had really hoped to get Rader at last!"

More of the pieces were falling into place as I listened to the Baroness' story. The pressure had been steadily building on Max Rader. He would have felt it, of course. Certainly he would have known he was being watched. But there hadn't been much he could do until Shikoku Hondo got out of prison. Hondo had the other half of the French key. So things had built up with a slow, inexorable pressure, until the valve popped. And now it *had* popped! In the dense gloom, I glanced down at my inner elbow, at the tiny AXE symbol glowing there. So much had gone before, so much patient work behind the scenes, so many people over so many years—watching and working and waiting. And now AXE was moving in for the kill!

In that moment, while I waited for the Baroness to continue her story, I knew that this was one of those cases where superficial indications could lead you astray, were in fact intended to lead you astray. Hawk hadn't told me everything about Mission Tiger. There was more to it— much more. But that was Hawk. Not that it mattered. I had a job to do, and I would do it. That was all that counted.

"So how did you find him again, with his new face?" I asked.

The Baroness laughed coldly. "He had *not* moved. Not sold his house, as I was told. If my constant watching worried him, then it also betrayed him. All he did was pretend to sell the house, to go away. He had his face altered. Then he returned as the new owner of the house."

"Clever," I admitted. "He sold his house to himself. Max Rader disappears and someone else moves into his house and takes up where Rader left off. What did he call himself when he came back?"

"Buddenbaum. Karl Buddenbaum. He was so clever about it. He was ill. High blood pressure. He had nothing to do with the neighbors. All his supplies were delivered. He never left the house except for an occasional stroll at night."

"His face was healing."

"Yes. So I knew afterward. But let me tell you how I spotted him. It was not one thing, but many. Many little things. I had watched him, spied on him for so long that I came to know all his little mannerisms. The way he bent over, the way he scratched his ear or rubbed his chin. The way he walked and stood. And it was this that betrayed him. Max Rader had done a little gardening. I had watched him often, through glasses from a room I rented nearby. On my last day in Hamburg, after I found out that Rader was gone, I went back to watch his house once more. I had an idea that he might come back.

"Rader did not come back. He had never gone. I watched the man calling himself Karl Buddenbaum working in the garden. Suddenly I knew it was Max Rader. The next day I followed him as he went downtown—it must have been his first time away from the house in weeks. I sat just across from him on a bus. I had a good look at him."

"And he at you," I said.

"He paid me no attention. And they had done a good job on his face—whoever they were. His own mother wouldn't have recognized him."

"Only you—of all the people in the world."

"Yes. Only me."

"I think he knows that," I said. "I think, dear Baroness, that we are going to have to take very good care of you until Max Rader is dead. I think that if this thing, Mission Tiger, hadn't broken exactly when it did, you might already be dead. You've been lucky. Hondo got out of prison in Tokyo and headed for Geneva. All sorts of pressures have been put on Rader. He hasn't found *time* to kill you yet. He's trying to get the gold tiger and run for it. With the tiger, *and* a new face, he'll be sitting pretty. Hondo has—or had—connections with the Japanese Commies. Maybe Rader was hoping to slip behind the Iron Curtain. But he can't afford to leave any loose ends behind. And you, baby, are a very loose end indeed."

"I know." She snuggled against me, her sleek, warm pelt dry now and beginning to arouse a new heat in me. I got up and pulled her to her feet. She came against me, her firm breasts mashed against my naked chest.

"No more," I said abruptly. "Not now. Work to do. Better go to your room. Lock the door. I'll see you in the morning. We're going to have a busy day."

The Baroness sighed. "If we must—but my little protectors? Can I have them back?"

"In the morning," I promised. "Come on. I'll take you to your room."

"But the food! I am starving. And the wine—we have not touched it. It is a fine wine—the Comtesse has a marvelous cellar. It is of the Hospice de Beaune."

"Fine." I picked up the lunch hamper and the bottle of wine from the cooler. "You drink it—in your room, with the door locked. Then go to sleep and don't worry. I'll be around."

She had slipped into the tiny golden bikini and her robe, dressing in the glow of my cigarette lighter. She was a delightful study in white and shadow, her breasts firm perfection as she bent over. Catching sight of a triangular swatch of honey-gold, I knew that she did not dye her hair. In the fragile, shadow-clotted gloom she once again looked so very young.

Again I felt the unfamiliar tenderness well up in me.

As I left her at her door I said, "You're positive that you will know Max Rader when you see him? If we see him?"

"I'll know him," she said fiercely. "I would know him in his grave!"

I kissed her goodnight. "Let's hope," I said, "that we see *him* there. Not you."

Eight

By nine o'clock the Villa Limbo slept. Or so it seemed. Taking no chances, I decided to wait until midnight before making my foray. There was plenty to occupy me in the meantime.

I recovered the fragment of French key and bound it securely in a plastic envelope not unlike a tobacco pouch. This I tucked into the waistband of my shorts, along with Hugo, while I completed certain other tasks.

From the rhino-hide suitcase I took a small vise, padded, and a small pair of pliers, also padded. I managed to affix the vise to the foot of my bed. I then fished the Baroness' little pistol out of Gladstone and went to work, wrenching and squeezing and tapping. I finished the job with a tiny hammer and put the tools and the Lilliput gun back in the suitcase.

I locked Gladstone and set the tear gas and alarm fixtures once more. I glanced at my watch. Time to go.

I fashioned a dummy of pillows and blankets in the bed and switched off the bedroom light. Then I waited on the little iron-railed balcony for fifteen minutes longer, hardly breathing.

Across the two hundred yards of water separating the villa from the mainland I could see scattered lights. Street lights, an occasional house, the clustered multicolored lights of what appeared to be a small fair or street carnival. Now and then the strains of a *carrousel* drifted over on the fitful breeze. Presently the music stopped and the colored lights blinked out.

The moon was gibbous, a little past the half, and intermittently masked by scudding clouds the color of elephant hide. There was an early autumn crispness in the air as I swung effortlessly down an ancient vine to the clump of oleander beneath the balcony. I darted across an expanse of open sward and spent another five minutes listening in a dark clump of pine. From this coign I studied the villa. Only a solitary light burned in the kitchens. Everything else was dark. Presumably—I couldn't help smiling—presumably Mignonne Franchette was asleep, dreaming her lascivious dreams. Osman the fat snored and regretted his long-departed manhood. The Baroness, satiated and replenished—God alone knew what went on in *her* devious mind!

I made for the wooden stairs leading down to the tiny dock. I moved like a phantom in the night, darting from tree to clump of brush, waiting for the swiftly moving cloud rack to obscure the burnished moon.

The dock was deserted, as I had expected. The aluminum skiff, tethered by its chain, moved and bumped against the piling.

I let myself into the water silently. It was warmer than the surrounding air. I slid under, the plastic envelope and cord ready in my hand.

Because of my yoga and constant breathing exercises, I could remain under water for nearly four minutes. I knew of only one man who could remain under water longer—a native pearl diver I had once met while on a mission in the Marquesas.

It took me less than two minutes to bind the plastic envelope securely to the foot of the piling. A good ten feet down beneath the breeze-riffled waters of Lac Léman. Let Max Rader find it there!

I had surfaced and was taking a deep breath when I saw it. The blinker light. It was winking furiously from the mainland, aimed at the island and the villa, a white flirtation in the night. I settled quietly by the dock, only my nostrils above water, and read the Morse.

The sender was using a regular blinker lamp, not a flashlight. The dots and dashes came in a smooth, practiced flow.

```
. .. ..    -.-. .- -.-. - . .-.    - .... . .-. . ..--..
```
I S   C A R T E R   T H E R E   ?

Yes, I murmured to myself. I am indeed here! Reading you loud and clear. I began to pull myself out of the water, my eyes searching the dark cliff overhead. Any second now—

There it was. From a clump of brush on the lip of the cliff, nearly directly over me, a bright little eye began to wink back at the far shore. At the foot of the stairs, I paused to read it. Whoever it was up there was not as expert as the sender on the mainland. The message, however, was brief. To the point.

```
-.-- . ...
```
Y E S

A tiny pause, then the blinker above me flickered a question mark at the shore.

```
..--..
```
?

I went up the wooden stairs four at a time, my bare feet making no sound. As I ran, I was thinking—fast. So they know who I am and where I am. At least one of them does—the sender in the bushes up there. But he doesn't quite know what to do with me. He needs instructions. I slipped Hugo out of my belt as I reached the last landing before the top of the cliff. The blinker on the mainland was working again.

```
-.. ---    -. --- -    .- .-.. .- .-. --
```
D O   N O T   A L A R M

I awaited the conclusion of the messages. I was within fifty feet of the bushes where the sender was concealed. I could afford to bide my time. Someone was going to be in for an unpleasant surprise when they started back to the villa. I smiled as I pressed the button on Hugo and heard the deadly little blade *snick* into position.

The light on the mainland flickered once more. WAIT FOR ORDERS. The sender in the bushes signaled an R .-. RECEIVED AND UNDERSTOOD -.- K — — —OUT

There was movement in the bushes now. I settled myself in the deepest shadow and waited. I could feel sweat beading my face. But it was a cool night, and I was not afraid. Then I understood why I was sweating so heavily—even KILLMASTER could revolt at the thought of thrusting a knife into soft, sweetly scented flesh that not many hours before he had kissed and caressed—

The moon escaped from the clouds. The sender came out of the bushes into the clear, limpid light. I breathed again, relief flooding over me. It was Osman, the fat eunuch. I would not have to kill a woman tonight.

Osman waddled across the lawn, his fat rippling, still dressed as he had been earlier. He carried the heavy box of a blinker lamp in one flabby hand. I stepped out of the shadows. I spoke softly.

"Osman. I want to talk to you."

The eunuch whirled with amazing speed. He dropped the blinker lamp and his hand darted toward a pocket in the ridiculous mountaineer's jacket. It came out with a knife. The long blade glinted evilly in the moonlight. This was a different Osman. There was no servility now, no groveling. The little eyes, swathed in fat, glared.

"So you spy on me, Mr. Carter? Ach—perhaps I was not careful enough. But I thought, I was sure, that after spending so much time in the arms of that harlot you would need rest. You would sleep. This is very bad, Mr. Carter. Very bad for me!"

The eunuch's voice was like a high flute wailing in the

night. The fat man held the switchblade straight before him, like a rapier, and began to circle me.

I circled counterclockwise, Hugo ready. I had already made my plan. Imperceptibly, I began to fall back, to retreat toward the rim of the cliff. There was one spot where it was clear, where the turf ran unobscured by trees or bushes straight to the cliff's edge.

Osman began to press his seeming advantage. He stopped circling and began moving slowly from side to side, always keeping his bulk between me and the villa, pressing me back to the rim of the cliff. Precisely what I wanted him to do.

I spoke for the first time since the knife duel had begun. "You're right, Osman. It *is* bad for you. If you kill me it will be even worse. Rader doesn't want me dead yet. I've got something he wants!" I watched the fat man's face intently as he spoke.

Osman frowned. He appeared worried even as he drove me back to the precipice.

"And if you don't kill me," I said with a grin, "I'll kill you! Looks like you're in a bind, fat boy! Even if you win, you lose!"

Osman cursed. He sprang with incredible speed, lancing the switchblade at my arm. I barely eluded the savage thrust. So that's it, I thought as I skipped back. He doesn't want to kill me! He's trying to disarm me, to wound me. Probably figures his weight will do the rest. And it might at that. Four hundred odd pounds of blubber.

Osman halted for a moment. The fat eunuch was beginning to breathe hard. He shrugged his massive shoulders. Fat rolled and rippled. Osman pulled off his jacket and wrapped it around his left forearm. The switchblade moved like a snake's tongue in his right hand.

Osman, the jacket rolled around his forearm as a shield, moved toward me again. "I think now I take care of you,

Mr. Carter. But you are right—I do not want to kill you. My master would not like that at all. I will wound you, disarm you, and then we shall see."

I skipped back out of range of the menacing switch-blade, shooting a swift glance back of me. Not far now. Perhaps twenty yards to the cliff's edge.

I began to taunt Osman. "You ball-less wonders always have a master, don't you? Or a mistress? Never your own man, are you? But then I was forgetting—you're *not* a man, are you?" I added a few choice opinions about Osman's sex life. They were as vile and obscene as I could make them.

The fat man rushed at me, stabbing furiously with the knife. "I am man enough to take care of you," he bellowed. He stooped and thrust the sword blade at my genitals. "I will make you like me!" Osman grinned. In the brilliant moonlight his teeth were yellow and rotten.

"When I finish with you, Mr. Carter, you will not be so much the great lover. That Baroness bitch will not sigh and moan so for your embraces. No woman will—ever!"

I gave the eunuch a mocking smile. "Why, Osman, I'm surprised at you! You're jealous!" As I spoke I feinted and circled sideways, wanting Osman to think I was trying to get back to the villa. The fat man leaped to bar the way. He glanced over my shoulder at the rim of the cliff and his blubbery little mouth creased in a smile of anticipation. He spat at me. "You cannot go far now," he gloated. "Soon you must stand and fight me. Then we will find out who is a man, Mr. Carter."

Still trying to enrage him, to make him lose his temper and so his guile and skill, I said: "Must we be so formal, fatso? You don't have to call me Mister. I'm not your master—yet! Later, maybe, after I skin some of that lard off you I'll let you kiss my feet and call me *Sahib!*"

Osman raised his rage-contorted face to the bright wheel of the moon. The fat man beseeched Allah to aid him in the destruction of this specimen of a diseased camel! I chuckled grimly. Osman was losing his temper, all right.

Time now to goad him a little more. Summoning all my grace, speed, and power, I leaped in. Hugo went *snickersnee* into plump flesh. Once, twice, three times I put the stiletto in up to the hilt, being careful to avoid vital spots. I wanted Osman alive as much as the fat man wanted *me* alive. Osman would talk—eventually.

I danced back out of range of the swooping knife. Osman roared with rage. Dark stains were leaking through his shirt. Yet he appeared not at all hurt. He came after me with renewed fury, stabbing low and bringing the switchblade up with a slashing twist of the wrist. I knew the stroke. You put your knife into your opponent's gut, low, then you ripped it across and up. The disemboweling stroke. Osman had forgotten his good intentions. And his orders. He was after my intestines now.

I moved in again. I stabbed twice with the stiletto, like a boxer with a good left jab, then was away before Osman could cut me. Blood smeared the entire front of the fat man now. The stiletto was stained and I felt the hot sticky stuff on my fingers. At that moment it occurred to me that I might be in a little trouble. There was something I hadn't counted on.

Osman's fat! There was so much of it. Hugo was deadly in ordinary circumstances, but the stiletto was not very long. I began to doubt if I *could* kill Osman with the stiletto, even if I wanted to. If I *had* to. But Hugo was all I had. Both Pierre and Wilhelmina were back at the villa.

I was very near the edge of the cliff now. It was not more than five feet behind me. Osman was panting heavily, his vast body leaking blood from a dozen wounds. He leered at me through a mask of blood and sweat. "Ha—so! Now where will you go, my friend? You will grow wings and fly away, perhaps?"

I pretended fear and weariness—so far I had gotten

no information from the fat man, no confirmation that he was indeed working for Max Rader. It must be true, of course, but I wanted proof. I had already assumed too much on this mission.

Now, as Osman panted in triumph and prepared for the last rush, I allowed myself to wilt, to droop with fatigue. "L—let's talk a minute," I gasped. "Wait—maybe we can work something out . . . you said yourself you didn't want to kill me!"

Osman himself was near exhaustion. Either that or the edge of his rage had dulled. "You are right. I do not. In fact, I am ordered not to harm you unless I have to. So if you will be sensible now—"

"You were ordered not to alarm me," I said. "But you have, Osman. You have." I held out a shaking hand. "See how you've alarmed me! But I forgive you, Osman. If I surrender will you promise not to kill me? Will you take me straight to Max Rader?"

The fat eunuch fell into the trap. "That I cannot do," he blurted. "I am only an underling. I merely work for Herr Rader. But he will come to see *you,* never fear—"

Osman broke off as he realized that I had tricked him into the admission. He wiped his bloody hands on his trousers and moved in toward me again. "So—you make tricks! All right. I, Osman, have had enough. I will kill you now and then make up the lie for Herr Rader. It will cost me much money, which I cannot afford, for Allah knows I am a poor man. But now you die—Carter!"

"You forgot the Mister," I taunted. "You're forgetting your manners, fat stuff!" I prepared for Osman's rush. I was counting on it. Then a deft sideways movement, a rolling block at the man's ankles, and Osman would be on his way over the cliff. I did not know precisely what lay beneath us at the bottom of the cliff. Rocks or deep water? It didn't matter too much. Osman *was* only an underling, wasn't he?

In any case, the Baroness and I would have to be on

our way. The Villa Limbo, obviously, was no longer a safe house.

But Osman did not rush me. Slowly, very slowly, he began to creep toward me. I began to worry a bit. I cursed under my breath. Osman was smarter than I had thought. Once those great, flabby, bleeding arms got me in a bear hug, I was going to be in real trouble!

By now I was at the very edge of the cliff. I risked one fast glimpse down, saw the glitter of moonlight on water. The drop was a good hundred feet.

To wait any longer might be fatal. With all my strength, I hurled Hugo at the fat man. The stiletto glinted as it flew through the air. It struck in Osman's massive belly and quivered there like a dart in a board.

Osman looked down at the knife still quivering in his living flesh, then he looked at me and laughed. "Ho—you think to kill Osman with a pin like that!"

The eunuch did not even bother to pluck the stiletto from his belly. He came for me, arms outspread, the switchblade cutting vicious swaths in the air. Osman was soaked in his own blood by now. He looked, I thought, like something from hell. And there was no time to lose.

I went forward in a great lunge. Eluding the fierce bite of Osman's knife, I caught the fat man's wrist in one hand. I had to keep that knife out of my guts.

Osman was grunting and slobbering like an enraged bear. His huge torso was slippery with blood. I clung desperately, holding the eunuch's knife away from me while I searched in the greasy folds of blubber for my stiletto. For Hugo, whose hilt was concealed by great, overlapping folds of fat and lard. I had the fleeting, absurd thought that if you boiled Osman down you would get a dozen barrels of oil.

I hung on grimly, still probing for Hugo, as the eunuch swung and swirled and cursed, trying to get his knife hand free, trying to brush me off as he would a flea.

We were struggling on the extreme edge of the cliff now.

I found the stiletto. The hilt was slippery with Osman's blood. I plucked the thin blade out, then plunged it in again. And again! Half a dozen times I rammed the stiletto into the eunuch's chest and belly. Blood spouted in fountains. Now I was as gory as Osman. And beginning to despair. It was like trying to kill a whale with a needle.

The fat man suddenly dropped his knife. He groped for my throat with both his dripping hands. In the bright moonlight his eyes were popping from his head, his mouth open in a feral snarl, his breath fetid in my nostrils.

"Maybe I die," the fat eunuch roared. "Maybe I die—but I take you too! Osman will not die alone!"

Who would have thought there was so much strength in the flabby hands? They were around my throat like an iron vise. Vainly I fought to free myself. I kept slamming the stiletto into blubber, as near the heart as I could manage, and began to twist the thin blade. Shove and twist! Twist and shove! I was hurting the giant now. Osman began to whimper, to moan, to emit little sobbing screams. But he clung to my throat like a huge bulldog.

I began to black out. I tried every trick in the book, but I could not break Osman's grip. The moon began to spin overhead, making silver pinwheels in the darkling sky. I felt my knees collapse. My hand was numb, without strength; I could no longer stab the fat man. Darkness was setting in—eternal darkness . . .

The lip of the cliff moved beneath our trampling feet, crumbling and tearing away. Osman and I went hurtling down into the void.

Not for a second during the long, tumbling, end-over-end fall did the eunuch let go his hold on my throat. And I was so near death that I did not really struggle any longer. The world was dark and full of pain and the agony was unbearable, without end, and yet must somehow be borne.

The shock of striking the water tore us apart. I went deep, retaining just enough sense to realize we had landed in deep water, not on rock, and that there was a chance I might still live. Feebly, I struggled away from Osman and struck for the surface.

It was the sweetest air ever breathed by man. I gulped it down in great sobbing lungfuls, feeling like a man who has been hanged and then cut down just before death. My throat was aflame; the pain of swallowing was intense.

I trod water and glanced around warily, waiting for Osman to surface. It seemed incredible, impossible, that the fat man could have any fight left in him. That he was still alive at all was a miracle. Yet—and here I had to admit a reluctant admiration—Osman had turned out to be a hell of a man. Balls or no balls, the fat eunuch had put on a show!

The moon flirted out from behind a little canopy of cloud. I saw it then, floating quietly near me, bobbing up and down with the gentle motion of the water. Osman's body. So Hugo had found a vital spot after all!

I had seen too many dead bodies to be fooled. Osman, still retaining a mass of air in his great carcass, floated face up, his sightless eyes staring at the mottled sky. He pitched and swayed in the currents like a huge dead fish.

I swam to the corpse, my strength flooding back now. I was beginning to think ahead, fitting bits and pieces into place, weighing pros and cons and ifs and but ;

I did not want to leave Osman for the police to find. Not immediately. The Baroness and I would be on our way soon, to find Max Rader—or to let Max find us— but in the meantime the police must be kept out of thi ;

I found Hugo buried deep in the dead flesh just ver the heart. My last despairing thrust had killed Osma. at last. I yanked the stiletto out, washed it in the water, then snapped it shut and put it back in the waistband of my trunks. Hugo had come through once more, though it had been a near thing. Now what to do with Osman's body?

I remembered the boathouse I had seen that afternoon. It had appeared unused, falling to pieces with sagging beams and scaling paint, but it would serve.

The boathouse was on the far side of the little dock. I worked my fingers into the flab beneath Osman's chin and began to swim, towing the fat corpse as a tug tows a liner. The task was surprisingly easy. Osman was nearly as buoyant as an inflated bladder.

I rounded the end of the little dock and approached the ancient boathouse. The bright moonlight was holding steady, etching every detail in silver and shadow. The boathouse was a bit larger than I had thought, built on slimy brick pilings and extending out over the water so that a fair-sized boat could be run directly into the shelter. Once there had been water doors, but these had long since rotted and fallen away. They lay ruined and aslant, pinioned only by a single rusty hinge each, like malformed teeth in the gaping mouth of the structure. I towed the dead man into the boathouse. Holes in the roof, where shingles had rotted away, let in the moonlight. Amid the ruin and desolation, the rot and neglect of time, the dirt and the cobwebs, I saw a couple of old canoes and a skiff. Broken paddles and sour-smelling pillows, chains and cordage, anchors and boat hooks and stiffened canvas and wood and ancient paint, mixed with stale water and dead fish.

And rats!

As I paused in the midst of the scummy water, treading and trying to decide what to do with the fat corpse, I saw and heard them. Dozens, perhaps hundreds of them. They rustled and squeaked from the rotten floor boards around the sides of the boathouse. They peered at me with little malevolent eyes, like red sparks in the half-gloom.

Bold bastards, I thought. They certainly don't seem much afraid of me.

At first I considered sinking the fat man, weighting

him down with some of the chains and small anchors lying about, but I decided it was no good. Osman was too buoyant. It would take a lot of weight, and time, to moor him securely to the bottom. I found a rope and made a noose for the fat man's neck. I tied the end of the rope to a rotting stair leading up from the water. I left the fat eunuch there, floating placidly at the end of his rope, staring through the holes in the roof. He would sink even tually, I knew, and it might be days, even weeks, before anyone entered the abandoned boathouse.

I swam rapidly back to the dock and pulled myself up. I had to get cracking. I had fully recovered from the ordeal with Osman by now. As I bounded up the stairs to the clifftop, I mentally blessed Purg for insisting that I have a body that was always in perfect condition. They knew their stuff, the lads at Purg, as hateful as they seemed.

Only the solitary kitchen light showed in the villa as I approached it. I glanced at the AXE Special on my wrist. Water could not harm it—nor blood. Now it said a few minutes past one. It might still be possible to catch a few hours' sleep before the Baroness and I left the island The blinker signals had told Osman not to alarm me, to await orders. That meant there was still a little time. The morning would bring problems, but they could be solved. Part of my creed was: anticipate trouble, count on it, but don't let it worry you too much. Sufficient unto the day the trouble thereof!

I did not go immediately to my room. Instead, I circled the villa until I was beneath the Baroness' window. It had an iron balcony very like the one on my own room. A trellis climbed the stucco wall near the balcony.

It took me but a moment to swarm up the trellis and peer into the bedroom. After a moment I could make out the form in the bed, covered only with a sheet, her amber-honey hair spread on the pillow. Softly I tried the window latch—the window was locked on the inside.

That meant nothing in itself, of course—she could have been out and back again and then locked the window.

I gazed at the trellis and thought not. Nothing for me, yet it would have been a job for her. She wasn't much of a climber, if the difficulty she'd had with the fire hose at the Hotel Lux was any indication. That had been genuine. No—if the Baroness had been out of her room tonight, if perhaps she had been working with Osman, then she had used the door. I would soon know.

A few moments later I was in the villa, examining the Baroness' bedroom door. The single, nearly invisible thread was unbroken. I had put it there after bidding her goodnight, looping it from the knob to a hinge. No one had been in or out of that door tonight.

I felt relief and contentment as I made my way to my own suite. I was beginning to think, even to hope, that the girl was on the level. Again I was conscious of my strange, unusual feelings of tenderness for the Baroness. Could it be that I—

Absurd! I put the thought away. This was not the time or the place for such thoughts. There never *would* be a time and place for such thoughts—not for KILL-MASTER! I lived in a different world—in a universe apart from ordinary men.

My suite was dark, as I had left it, but the moment I stepped inside I knew something was amiss. A moment later I knew what it was. I could smell her.

I heard the bed creak. She was awake and waiting for me.

Softly, I said, "Mignonne? Just what in hell do you think you're doing in my bed?"

Mignonne Franchette laughed out of the darkness. "That is a silly question, M'sieur Nick. You *know* what I am doing in your bed. We both know, is it not? I am waiting for you, my big one. Most impatiently. I am waiting. Now we will cease this foolish talking and you will come to bed and give Mignonne what it is she wants, *non?*"

"*Non!* I'm very tired, Mignonne. I must sleep. Be a good girl and have a heart. Scram back to your own room." Her scent was heavy in the room. I could visualize her plump, white body waiting beneath the covers. A bovine type, this determined little peasant girl. She knew what she wanted. And, as the old song went—she wanted what she wanted when she wanted it!

But I was definitely not in the mood. "Nothing doing," I said curtly. "Beat it, now. We'll just forget this ever happened, Mignonne. Just be a good girl and clear out, huh?"

She giggled. "I am *not* a good girl, M'sieur Nick. I do not wish to be a good girl. I wish only for you to make love to me! To make the great love to poor Mignonne. I am most discreet, M'sieur, as I have said before. Why do you hesitate, my handsome one? Nobody will ever know. I will not tell. I will not bother you again if you do not wish it. But for now I insist that you come to bed and make love to Mignonne. If you do not, M'sieur, I will begin to scream. I can scream very loud. *Formidable!* I will scream until the Baroness comes, and then I will accuse you of rape. It is not pretty, *oui?*"

I felt like yanking her out of bed and smacking her plump behind. Yet I was amused. This kid had an extremely bad case of hot panties. I wondered if she knew anything about the late Osman? It was doubtful, yet . . .

Mignonne's next words resolved matters for me.

"If you are not kind to Mignonne," she said, "I will tell the police that you fought with Osman! That you killed him!"

Silence. Then I said, "How do you know about that?"

She giggled again. "I saw you. I watched you fighting in the moonlight, *mon brave.* You were *magnifique.* I am glad you killed him, though I do not understand why. He was a horrible pig! *Cochon*."

I was wary. "How do you know I killed him?"

I could almost see her shrug in the dark. "You fell over the cliff together, *non?* You were fighting the most terrible, each trying to kill the other, *oui?* You alone return! So the fat one is dead! *Alors!* So who cares, *chéri?* Come now to Mignonne. The night will not last forever."

I imitated her Gallic shrug. When the Fates conspired, what could you do? I had not the slightest doubt that unless I climbed into bed with her, Mignonne would keep her word and start screaming. That I could explain to the Baroness—not that I owed her any explanation. The cops were a different matter. I didn't want Osman found just yet.

I went toward the bed. "You are a character," I told the maid. "You are also a blackmailer. I predict that one day you are going to get into a lot of trouble."

As I stood beside her in the dark, I slipped Hugo out of my trunks and beneath the mattress where I could reach the stiletto in a hurry. Hawk, I thought, really couldn't object to this particular horizontal episode. I *was* protecting Mission Tiger.

Hands came out of the dark and began to fuss with my trunks. The scent of Mignonne, perfume and body, filled the little room. She reached for my legs and pulled me down beside her on the bed.

She whispered into my ear, "Oh *chéri!* You make me so happy! You will see, my big one! Mignonne is going to do *everything* to you!"

Her arms, soft and plump and sweet-smelling, entwined about my body. With surprising strength, she wrestled me beneath her. Her melon-heavy breasts were cool on my chest.

I sighed and relaxed. It was not unpleasant, not at all. For a man who had been so close to death just a few minutes before, this was rather like emerging from a tomb. That it meant nothing but the temporary appeasement of animal desires was not important. In a few hours the dawn would come again, bringing with it new problems and new perils. In the meantime—

I grinned in the dark. To paraphrase that ancient sage, Confucius: when rape is inevitable, relax and enjoy it.

Nine

When I awoke I was alone. Mignonne had kept her whispered promise to be discreet. I could smell coffee, and from below there was a faint clatter of dishes. My watch said a little after seven. High time to be up and going. Running!

But running into danger, not away from it.

At breakfast the Baroness was radiant. She wore gray slacks and a heavy, cable-stitched green sweater that went well with her darkened honey hair. She wore little make-up, and her gray eyes sparkled. She did have a patrician beauty, I admitted to myself, sipping my coffee. This morning she was regal.

I hurried through breakfast. Mignonne hovered, all smiles, and I found it difficult to avoid her eye. Her desires temporarily appeased, Mignonne was like a plump little pigeon trying to show her gratitude. She kept my coffee cup overflowing. There was no chance for any meaningful conversation with the Baroness. If she was aware of any of the night's events, she said nothing. It was much too early for her to miss Osman, or to wonder.

After breakfast I winked at the beaming Mignonne and followed the Baroness out to the terrace. It was another sunny day, enameled with the hard, blue-and-gold sheen of early autumn. Some of the leaves were just beginning to turn.

I wasted no time. "We're going fishing," I told the Baroness. "Just you and me. We'll row out into the lake in the skiff and try to pick up a boat of some sort. We won't be coming back, so take everything you'll need. Maybe it would be a good idea to pack your stuff in that lunch hamper—it will make it look better. We're going fishing, and we're taking along a lunch. Be careful. Act as natural as you can. I'm pretty sure we're being watched from the mainland. Now get started—this place is dangerous now. We're on the run again."

Her eyes were wide with surprise. "But Nicky—I do not understand. I thought—"

"Never mind what you thought," I snapped. "I thought this was a safe house too, but I was wrong."

I decided to give it to her with brutality, the full shotgun blast, and watch for a reaction.

I said: "Osman was Rader's man. Rader knows we're here. I caught Osman signaling last night and killed him."

Watching her as a falcon watches a pigeon, I had to admit that she was one of two things—genuinely surprised or the world's greatest actress. I did not yet know which. That was the hell of it—I did not know which!

Elizabeth von Stadt went very pale at my disclosure. She nibbled at her lower lip and put one hand to her breast, a habit she had in times of agitation. Her voice trembled, was unsure, when she finally spoke. "Osman? Y—you killed Osman?"

"I had to," I said. "He was trying to kill me. He damned near succeeded, too. Eunuch or not, he was a rough sonofabitch. And he was Rader's man. Planted here."

I almost added—planted here so very conveniently at the Villa Limbo. Step into my parlor, said the spider to the fly. And yet I could have sworn that she was shocked and surprised. I had caught a lot of liars in my day, and to my experienced eye the Baroness' surprise seemed genuine.

Finally she said: "I—I just can't understand it. Osman,

of all people. Why, he's been with the Comtesse for years. She would have trusted him with her life."

"Maybe *she* could," I said curtly. "We couldn't. Somehow or other Max Rader got to him. I don't understand it either, and there's no time now—get your stuff together and join me down at the dock in fifteen minutes. Don't forget—we're being watched. Okay. Fifteen minutes."

As she was turning away, she said, "Perhaps I should have my little knife and gun back now? Please?" Her red lips curled into a little smile. "I might have to fend for myself, you know."

"Come on," I said. I led the way to my room. I dug the little pistol and stiletto out of Gladstone and handed them to her. "There you are, kid. Loaded for bear. But you won't have to use them—I'll look after you."

"Until this thing with Rader is over, at least?"

She came close to me, putting her body against mine from shoulder to knee. With the stiletto in one hand, the pistol in the other, she put her arms around my neck. Her big eyes were full of lavender shadows. Her lips brushed mine. "You are so all business again this morning, my Nicky! You frighten me a little, I think. You—you have not forgotten so soon what happened? I have not. I never will!"

I kissed her, and she clung to me. After a moment I pushed her away gently. "I haven't forgotten, baby. But I killed a man last night, remember? Right now we're in a pretty hot spot. So let's save it, shall we? When this is over there will be plenty of time for us."

The Baroness laid a finger on my lips. "Do not promise. I hate promises. They are always broken. I will meet you at the dock in fifteen minutes."

It was not much of a ruse, I had to admit, but it was all we had. With my rhino-hide bag and the lunch hamper in the little aluminum skiff there was little freeboard. I had to row the skiff with great caution to prevent foundering, even in the placid waters of Lac Léman.

The illusion of fishing was aided by a couple of rods that Mignonne had managed to produce from a store-room. I had had a moment alone with the maid in the kitchen, during which she had insisted on kissing me and fumbling with my fly. I finally managed to extricate my-self and left, thinking that, unfortunately, Mignonne Franchette was going to be lonely tonight when the Baroness and I did not return.

I rowed, keeping hard at the task until we were well out into the lake. The lake was only about four miles wide here, so there was no question of escaping observa-tion from the shore, unless the watchers were careless, or I could keep the island between themselves and the watchers. But I couldn't count on that.

The problem was solved, as best it could be, by the increasing lake traffic. As the morning wore on we found ourselves in the steamer lanes. People on the decks stared at us as the white pleasure boats huffed past, kicking up waves that caused the little skiff to rock dangerously.

"We'll be damned lucky if we don't have to swim for it," I told the Baroness. "One more wave like that last one and we've had it."

She was sitting on the stern seat, precisely in the middle, carefully balancing herself. In the bottom of the skiff was the lunch hamper and the rhino-hide suitcase. We had thrown the fishing rods away.

"It might be a good idea," the Baroness said now, "if we could fake a drowning. The police would find the overturned boat and the oars—no sign of our bodies, you know! It would be in the papers. We might even fool Rader and his men. At least we would gain a little time."

"I doubt we would fool Rader," I said. "But it isn't a bad idea. First, though, we've got to have somewhere to go. We don't want to make it *too* real."

I stopped rowing and glanced around. In the distance, I could see a white lake-steamer heading for us. That was no good. A steamer wouldn't stop unless we were *really* in trouble. And there would be too many questions. What we needed was a private boat. A rental launch, empty for the moment, or—I spotted the scarlet triangle of a sailboat not far away. There were always a number of the lateen-rigged little craft on the lake in fair weather. That could be the answer.

We both noticed it at the same time. Fog! A dampish white mist, clammy and cold, dropping over the lake like a shroud. It came suddenly, out of nowhere, blanketing the sun. At the same time the wind began to rise with a slow but insistent pressure. Water that had been a pellucid blue now turned a nasty gray, showing small white teeth.

"It's the *molan*," the Baroness said. "A fall storm. I have seen them before. We'd better get off the lake, Nicky, or we'll be in real trouble."

"I couldn't agree more." I gazed through the fast-thickening mist. One of the lateen-rigged craft was making a tack, heading for home, and would pass close to us. I picked up the oars and began to row furiously, setting a course that would intercept the sailboat. No need to worry about watchers now. The fog took care of that.

At my hail the boat dropped its sail and came about, rolling and pitching in the rising sea. The occupants of the boat, a young man and a girl, both tanned and looking enormously strong and healthy, helped the Baroness aboard. I pitched Gladstone and the lunch hamper after her and leaped nimbly aboard. As I did so I managed to overturn the aluminum skiff. We left it floating forlornly, attended by drifting oars, as the young skipper hoisted his sail and we got under way. The wind was much stronger now, the little craft heeling far over as we ran in a long tack down the lake toward Geneva.

"Let me do the talking," I told the Baroness in English. "You'd better get below and wait for me. I'll give them a good story and a wad of francs. I think our luck's holding."

The Baroness smiled and went down the companionway to a tiny cabin. I went aft, where the young fellow and the girl were huddled together in the cockpit. They were good-naturedly curious about this crazy American and his lady—in the middle of Lac Léman in a skiff while the *molan* was blowing! *Sacré bleu!* It is to wonder at their sanity!

I told them an outrageous lie about running off with the wife of another man. The husband was a beast, naturally, while we were true lovers. I was sure they would understand, *non?* And they would undertake to put us ashore in Geneva and hold their tongues, *oui?*

They believed the wad of francs I pressed on them, if not my story, and I left them struggling with the tiller while the little craft hissed through the water. We would, the young man said, make Geneva harbor in a couple of hours, if the luck was with us. I went below to the little cabin. The Baroness, her lithe body supine on a narrow bunk, was smoking and staring at the low ceiling. I kissed her red mouth lightly, then sank onto the opposite bunk.

"Looks like we might make it," I said as I lit my own cigarette. "This storm was a break. Max Rader will have to waste a little more time locating us again. He'll do it, of course."

She blew smoke across the little cabin at me. "Is that not the idea, Nicky? You want to meet him now, don't you? Want him to come out into the open? So I can—how do you say it—finger him for you?"

I nodded. "True. But I want to meet him on my own ground, at a time of my own choosing. He must guess that, of course, and he'll try to avoid playing it my way. What I can't understand is why he hasn't made a move before now. He's waiting. For what? Osman was told not to alarm me. Why? I get the idea that Rader is biding his time, waiting for something to happen. Something I don't know about. I wish I did."

"There really has not been very much time, Nicky. Things have been happening so very fast! Perhaps Max

Rader needs time to get organized. Things change so fast!"

"Maybe." I listened to the hiss and gurgle of water just outside the cabin. Just a quarter of an inch of fragile hull separated us from the lake.

For a moment there was silence in the cabin, then the Baroness sighed. "I have been very patient, my Nicky. Do you not agree?"

I looked at her inquisitively. "Patient about what?"

She made a little *moue* and clasped her hands together. "About everything, darling! Everything! This golden tiger, the thing you found in the false teeth—ugh—and now you tell me you had to kill Osman. I am perishing with curiosity, Nicky. Oh, I know I am only an agent working for you and AXE. I am only a temporary. But I would like to know *why* we do all these things, *non?* Please, Nicky? We have time now. Tell me a little of what goes on?"

For a moment I considered it. Hawk had warned me not to tell her more than was necessary. So I wouldn't. Yet I could see no harm in giving her the background of Mission Tiger. She probably couldn't make much sense of it anyway.

I told her what had transpired during my day-long briefing in Washington, four days earlier.

The Thinkers, the Brain Boys of AXE, had been working on Mission Tiger for years. A hard core of fact and a lot of educated guessing had gone into their final analysis and recommendation for action.

Viz.: The golden tiger with the ruby eyes had been stolen by the Japanese from a temple in what was now part of Indonesia. Colonel Shikoku Hondo had been the prime thief. Shortly afterward, another colonel had arrived in the Far East—Colonel Max Rader, an SS colonel assigned personally by Hitler to foster good relations between the Japanese and the Germans.

The Japanese were equally anxious to ingratiate

themselves with the Third Reich. After all, if they were going to share the world between them, they would have to get along.

Some Japanese brain conceived the idea of making Hitler a present of the golden tiger. When Colonel Rader returned to Berlin, he took the tiger with him. He also was accompanied by Colonel Shikoku Hondo, now assigned to permanent liaison in the German capital.

Hitler, though pleased with the gift, was no art lover. He gave the tiger to his fat air marshal, Hermann Goering, who appreciated the finer things of life.

Fat Hermann, as all the world knew, was a cunning and greedy man. And a cautious man. Early in the war he had made arrangements for the Swiss to permit him to rent a vault in the bank of Paul Chardet et Fils.

Here the Baroness broke into my story. "But how could Goering do that? The Swiss are so stubborn and upright—so *neutral*. It isn't like them to let themselves be blackmailed."

I lit another cigarette. "The Brains say it happened— that Goering offered to release five thousand Jews from the camps if the Swiss would play ball. If they didn't, he threatened to make the thing public. You can see that he had the Swiss over a barrel. So they went along and let him have his bank vault. Everything very hush-hush, of course, and everybody reasonably happy. Goering had a hiding place for his loot, and the Swiss got credit for saving five thousand Jews."

As the war went on Goering began to accumulate more and more loot. He used Max Rader, now a general in the SS, to convey the treasure to the vault in Switzerland. Sometimes Shikoku Hondo, still a colonel, would accompany the German.

Hermann Goering did not send the golden tiger to Switzerland until the early spring of 1945, when he was sure the war was lost. It was the last trip made by Max Rader as courier, and this time he was accompanied by

Hondo. And this time the two men had decided to double-cross Goering.

"Rader must have known it was the last chance," I explained. "Goering had ordered him to seal the vault and bring back the French key. The Brain Boys think that Rader obeyed orders—up to a point. They also think that he and Hondo switched keys! They gave Goering a phony and kept the real key themselves. Because they didn't trust each other, they cut the half key in half again. Each kept a piece. They planned to get together after the war and split the fat boy's treasure between them. Only it didn't quite work out that way. Hondo was tried for war crimes—he liked to chop off GI heads, it seems—and he was lucky to get only thirty years!"

"Rader got off free," said the Baroness bitterly. "Damn him."

"But Hondo hadn't," I went on, "and that messed up the whole thing for Rader. With Hondo in prison there wasn't a thing he could do but wait. Now the waiting is over. Hondo served twenty years of his time, then, last week in Tokyo, they let him out. He made a beeline for Geneva, and all the machinery started to move. A lot of people, not only AXE, have been waiting for those bastards to go after the tiger. It's taken a lot of time and patience and money and men to get to this point. That's why they handed the final phase to AXE. They can't afford to have anything go wrong now."

I leaned from the bunk to stub out my cigarette in an ash tray. There was only the sound of the storm around us, and the creak and groan of the little boat as she battled it.

Elizabeth von Stadt had twisted on her bunk to face me. She cupped her small, well-shaped chin in her hand and stared across at me. It was gloomy in the little cabin. Her eyes had an odd glint.

"You're going to kill Max Rader, aren't you? You've meant to from the start. That's why they sent an AXE man. Your government wants the tiger, but they don't want any fuss or bother. No loose ends. No questions asked by anyone, anywhere, anytime. That's it, isn't it?"

"I can't tell you much more," I said. "You're right, in a way. *Your* people, the West Germans, want the loot in Goering's vault. The Indonesians want their tiger back. We want to give it to them and look like a good uncle— make a little political hay in the Orient. God knows we can use it! Aside from that, both Rader and Hondo are war criminals and nobody is going to miss them or care what happens to them. Tough for them, maybe, but they don't deserve any better." I shrugged. "Hondo cut off GI heads, Rader was in the SS. It's only an evening of scores."

"And you're the executioner." Her eyes were wide, fixed on me with a strange intensity. Her long, beautiful body moved slightly on the bunk. I sensed that she was becoming excited. Some women, I knew, were affected that way by violence. Even by tales of violence.

Abruptly, I tried to change the subject. "I'm not an executioner," I told her. "I'm an AXE agent, that's all. I have permission to kill—at my own discretion. I never *do* kill unless I absolutely have to."

She stared at me for a long time. Something about her eyes made me uneasy, but at the same time they began to arouse me.

Softly, very softly, the Baroness said: "Come over here, Nicky."

Ten

It was well after noon when the sailboat made Geneva harbor. The *molan* had begun to subside as suddenly as it had blown up. Sun sparkled once more on diminishing wavelets. Near the Quai du Mont Blanc the fountain in the harbor spewed a column of milky foam two hundred feet into the air, the spray forming myriad little rainbows as it fell.

Carrying the rhino-hide bag and the luncheon hamper, I urged the Baroness away from the quay as fast as possible. I didn't think we had been spotted, but we could take no chances.

"I've got to leave you for a little while," I explained, "but you'll be okay." I did not mention the *dépôt*. As we turned into the Rue Gaston my brain was busy with the plan I had been formulating just before the Baroness had turned into quite another sort of tiger than the one we had been discussing.

A tiger of flesh. This one, I admitted, as we hurried through the busy streets, was really insatiable.

I left her on a bench in the Civic Gardens, the lunch hamper beside her. "You'll be fine," I assured her. "Just look like you're expecting someone to share a picnic lunch. You're fretting because they're late. Put on a little act if any cops get curious. They won't, though. You look too respectable. If the worst comes up—well, you've got your little friends in your garters." I glanced down at her

119

lovely legs, slim in the gray slacks. "You have, I suppose?"

She squeezed my arm. "I have. But I hope I don't have to use them. Hurry back to me, my Nicky."

"As fast as I can." We stopped and I bought a bag of peanuts from a vendor. I handed it to her. "Here. Feed the pigeons. Help kill the time."

After I left her I walked through a department store, lost myself in the milling mob of shoppers, and left by a side door. I changed cabs twice, then walked the last six blocks. As I entered the fleabag building where the *dépôt* was housed I was certain—as certain as an AXE man ever could be—that I had not been tailed. I smiled as I dived down the gloomy stairs leading to the sub-basement. If my thinking was right they wouldn't be interested in me at the moment. Not *me*.

Five minutes later I was talking to Hawk in Washington. Briefly, succinctly, I told him everything that had happened. Hawk listened without comment or interruption.

When I finished, Hawk said: "You fell in and came up smelling like a rose, my boy. But we're not out of the woods yet. Not by a long shot."

"You're mixing your metaphors, sir." I chuckled. "But I see what you mean. But if I'm not out of the woods—I'm at least halfway in! The only way I can go now is *out*. Rader has got to make a move pretty soon. In the meantime, I'd like you to run a check on a Comtesse de Lanquoc. *Lang-ock,* yes, that's it. She lives in Paris. Used to be a pretty famous concert pianist."

"Will do." Hawk cleared his throat. "Anything else I should know? How are you and the Baroness von Stadt getting on?"

"I'll get to her in a minute," I said. I meant to save that for last, because Hawk was probably going to blow his top.

"You'd better call off the watch on the bank," I told

the boss. "Call off the border watch, too, and all the auxiliary agents. I won't need them now, and they might alarm Rader, scare him into doing something I don't want him to do. I've got to weasel him out into the open, and I can do it better alone. That's the thing that bothers me most—the way he's just sitting back and waiting, as though he had all the time in the world. I don't like it at all. The guy's smart and he seems to have quite an organization. The more time he has, the tougher he's going to be to take. I've got to get him out where I can hit him!"

"Hmmmmm—" Hawk seemed doubtful. I could visualize him sitting at his desk, lean and spare, chewing on the eternal cigar (which he never bothered to light), his shrewd old brain clicking like a computer.

"You're sure you want to go it alone?" Hawk was still doubtful.

"Yes. I think it's best that way. Remember, I've got Hondo's half of the key. Rader has to have that key or he's out of luck. He's *got* to come out in the open sooner or later. As I say, I'm a little worried because he hasn't made a move yet. But he will—maybe very soon. I—I'm trying a little game of bait the hook." Here it came. Hawk might not like what he was going to hear next.

"What do you mean, bait the hook?" Hawk's voice was dry, questioning. I could imagine his ears twitching.

"I'm using the Baroness for bait. I left her in the Civic Gardens. I'm pretty sure we were followed there, but I didn't tell her. If they grab her, and I think they will, then we're on our way."

A long silence. Over the scrambler I could hear Hawk clearing his throat again. That really must have jarred his old cigar.

Then: "You've got carte blanche, N3. You know that, of course." I grinned. Hawk only called me N3 when he was displeased.

Hawk went on. "In my opinion it's too risky. She's an

agent on loan from a friendly power. In a sense we're responsible for her. I wouldn't have approved it."

"There wasn't time to ask you," I said glibly. "And as you say, sir, I have carte blanche. I think it'll work."

"But in giving them the girl you've given them a club over you."

"No, sir. At least I don't look at it that way. I've simply established a go-between. I don't think Rader will hurt the girl—not at first."

Hawk coughed. "When she is the *only* one who knows his new face? You think he's going to let her live?"

"No," I admitted. "I don't. I think he intends to kill her."

"Then how in hell—" Hawk was beginning to sputter.

"It won't come to that," I promised. "I got her in—at least I hope I have—and I'll get her out. Alive."

"You sound damned sure of yourself, boy!"

"No more than usual," I said. "Look, sir, look at how it figures. Rader isn't going to worry about the girl, or anything else, until he gets the other half of the French key. He's *got* to have that or all his scheming and stealing, plus twenty years of waiting, have all been for nothing. And to get the key he's got to deal with me. He knows I won't deal if he does anything to the girl. Another thing is that time is running out for Rader—the girl tells me they're getting ready to try him for war crimes again. And Swiss banks don't hold deposits forever. I don't know the law, but I think it's getting close to the time when the bank can seize whatever is in that vault Rader must know all that. He's in a bind. I'm his only hope! He's got to get the key from me—and to do that he's got to show himself. When he does, I'll kill him and take *his* half of the key, and you can get your bloody tiger and ship it back to Indonesia and we can make like the benevolent uncle. I don't think it's going to buy us anything—but that isn't my province."

"I'm glad you appreciate that fact, N3." Hawk's voice

was a bit cold. "And just for the record, I want to repeat what you were told at the briefing—our State Department wants first look at the tiger. So if you should happen to get your hands on it—other than taking it out of the bank vault in the ordinary way, of course—just remember that State gets first look!"

"Understood," I said. "I know there's more to this deal than you're telling me, sir. And that's okay with me—the less I know the less I can spill if the going gets tough. I'm not one of the cyanide boys, you know." I had always scorned the little death pellets that some AXE agents carried. I had always believed that a good agent ought to have enough confidence in his own wits and strength never to have to consider suicide.

Hawk's tone was very dry now. "I'm glad to hear that you approve of the way we're running things back here, N3. I'm sure the President will be happy to hear it, too. And if it will make you feel any better, only three people know the *real* reason we want that tiger. Myself, the Secretary of State, and the President of the United States. Now—anything else?"

"Yes, sir. I'll need a car. Right away. One of the Jags will suit best, I think."

"Right. Requisition one from the *dépôt* there. I'll okay it later. That it?"

"That's all. I'm on my way. If my little bit of honey works and I draw some flies—well, I should be able to clean this thing up in a matter of hours. Just please remember—unless I yell for help I don't want any interference! I've got to do it my own way."

"Understood. Good luck, boy. And—Nick . . ."

"Sir?"

"Be careful."

"I will. Good-bye, sir."

I made arrangements with the men on duty at the *dépôt* to leave a Jaguar in the Excelsior Hotel parking lot in an hour. The AXE cars were usually new, but carefully treated to look old and scruffy. Tires, made especially for AXE, were bulletproof, as were the windows and the specially made bodies. AXE did not go in for a lot of gimmicks, but there was the usual radar and radio hooking into the AXE European network.

I was whistling as I left the *dépôt* and made my way back to the Civic Gardens. The Baroness would *not* be waiting, I hoped. I was sure we had been tailed from the quay, as I had expected. I had pretended otherwise to the girl, but I was certain that I had spotted the tail. A fat little guy in a leather windbreaker and a Trilby hat.

It figured. I had not really expected to lose Rader's men by rowing out onto the lake. The sudden storm wouldn't have fooled them much either. They would count on the Baroness and me being picked up. There would remain only the question of our destination. Max Rader obviously had plenty of men—he would have covered every possible port.

As I neared the spot where the Baroness was supposed to be waiting, I hastened my pace, creating the impression of an anxious man in a hurry. The act would have to be good to fool Rader—*if* he was fooled.

I reached the spot and glanced around. No Baroness. Good. They had her, then. They would have done it very skillfully and professionally, I was sure. She would have had no chance to create a disturbance, much less use her little weapons. That had worried me a bit. If the Baroness put up a fight, if she screamed or fought them or in any way attracted the attention of the police, the ruse would have failed. The whole deal would have been a mess. Rader's men would have gotten scared and beat it. The Baroness would probably have been jailed. And Rader and I would still be stalemated.

So it was with a deep sense of inner satisfaction that I paced to and fro before the bench where I was to have rejoined the Baroness. I put on my distraught act, frowning and rubbing my chin nervously, glancing around with a puzzled expression. I lit a cigarette and took a few nervous puffs, then cast it away. I was conscious of being watched now. By whom I didn't know yet, but the sensation was there. I could feel the eyes somewhere in the milling, passing throng. I was hardly ever wrong about that. When I was being watched I got an itchy feeling along my spine. I had it now.

I waited for ten minutes, peering anxiously at every woman who passed. I was expecting the Baroness and I was going to give her hell when she returned from straying. Now and then I kicked Gladstone peevishly.

Finally, when I was sure the watcher had gotten the idea, I turned and strolled slowly out of the gardens. I walked like a puzzled man, deep in thought.

I made for the center of town. Fifteen minutes later, I checked into the Excelsior Hotel, paying in advance, refusing to let the boy carry the heavy Gladstone bag.

The elevator was an old one, an open cage in the Continental style. Just as it slid upward, I saw the man in the Trilby hat enter the hotel and approach the desk. It wouldn't be long now. I grinned. I had signed my own name in bold black ink on the register: *Nicholas Carter*. Laying it right on the line for Max Rader. The next move was up to him.

While I had been at the *dépôt* the rhino-hide suitcase had been restocked. I now had clean clothing and other necessities of a more deadly nature. While I waited, I took a leisurely shower. The call would come. I was sure of it. I hummed as I shaved.

I had just completed my yoga for the day when the phone tinkled. I picked it up.

"Yes?"

"Mr. Carter? Mr. Nicholas Carter?" The voice was a low tenor, firm and commanding.

I grinned and flicked the ash from my cigarette. "Yes,

I'm Nicholas Carter. Is this General Rader?" Never hurts to use titles or rank, I figured. The most astute of them can be buttered up.

There was a long silence, broken only by a humming on the wire. Then the voice said: "I am General Max Rader, yes. Or I was. I am flattered that you remember my former rank, Mr. Carter."

"Nothing at all," I said cheerfully. "We've got quite a file on you, General. *Quite* a file."

"I'm sure you have, Mr. Carter. But let us get on. I did not call to exchange amenities. I will be very brief—and if you have made arrangements to trace this call, don't bother. It would lead you only to a public phone."

"I figured that," I said, "so I didn't bother. What's on your mind, General?" As though I didn't know!

"I will be most succinct, Mr. Carter. I have the girl— the Baroness von Stadt. You probably guessed that?"

"I did, yes. It was careless of me to leave her, but I thought we had lost your people for the time being. I was wrong." I let concern and the beginnings of anger seep into my voice. "Don't hurt her, General. I wouldn't like that. I'm warning you—I'm holding you personally responsible for her safety!"

Rader grunted harshly. "I look forward to seeing you, Carter. I do indeed. I have heard a great deal about you and have discounted most of it as mere myth and lies. But what they say about your effrontery appears to be true. *You* are in no position to bargain, my dear sir. Not if you care anything about the Baroness."

"Oh, but I do, General. I care a lot about the Baroness. That's why I'm warning you. Don't harm her. Besides, that should be unnecessary. I think we can perhaps do our business without anyone getting hurt."

Another pause. I grinned at the phone. I was upsetting Max Rader's preconceived ideas, and the creep was having a little trouble figuring it out.

Then: "You are willing to bargain, then? To exchange the girl for—for what I want?" Rader's English was good, with just a hint of the Teuton.

"It depends," I said. "I hate to just bargain with a character like you—I'd much rather just kill you out of hand. But I do have carte blanche in this matter, and if I have to bargain I will. And I seem to have made a bad mistake. You've got me over a barrel, General. I want the girl back."

Rader laughed. "You are an honest man, at least. I can well believe that you would like to kill me. I shall see to it that you do not have the chance. As for the bargain —maybe we can do business. But I warn you, Carter. I most emphatically warn you—no tricks!"

I affected just a hint of weariness and defeat. "As you say, General, I am really in no position to bargain. I just hate to get licked by a bastard like you. But if I must, I must—what's your proposition?"

"I have reason to believe that you have Colonel Hondo's half of the French key," said Rader. "I want it. In return I will give you the girl safe and unharmed."

"It isn't enough," I said. "I've got to salvage something out of this deal or my name is mud. I've pulled a hell of a rock as it is, and I've got to worry about my own skin. I can let you get away with the tiger—though my people aren't going to like it a damned bit—but I'll have to have the rest of the stuff in the vault. All of Goering's loot. If I can salvage that, maybe they won't shoot me. What do you say, General? I get the girl and everything else in the vault. You get the tiger and a good head start."

Rader was silent for so long that I began to feel anxious, afraid I had overplayed my hand. I couldn't hope to convince the man that I was absolutely on the level—at least not over the phone. But I did hope to insinuate just a sliver of doubt into Rader's mind—that there was just a *chance* that I *might* be on the level.

The real weakness in my position, in the whole setup, was the ease with which they had gotten the girl. I knew that and was afraid of it. Yet so far it seemed to have slipped past Rader. He appeared to accept the fact that I had really made a bad mistake.

Finally Rader spoke again. "We have spoken enough over the phone," he said briskly. "Too much. We must resolve this face to face, Carter. So you will return to the Villa Limbo and wait. That is all. Wait. I will get in touch with you in due time. And remember—no tricks! Or you will never see the Baroness von Stadt alive again "

"And you," I said mildly, "will never get Hondo's half of the French key. And speaking of your nasty little partner—what happened to his body? The police are keeping very quiet about it."

Max Rader laughed again, this time with genuine humor. "The police do not know about Hondo. And he is not dead!"

"Damn!" I muttered. "I *am* losing my touch."

"I have the Colonel," Rader went on, "and I will take care of him in due course. But let us not talk of Hondo—he is of no importance now."

"Yes," I agreed. "I can see that. Without his half of the key he wouldn't be of much importance. I think I foresee a watery grave for the Colonel, huh?" Cheerfully, I added, "Be sure you use plenty of weight, General. We don't want him popping up in the lake and embarrassing everybody."

"Hondo is a fool and deserves what he will get," Rader grunted. "Now enough—go to the *villa* and wait."

"Roger," I said. "Wilco—oh, I suppose I should tell you—I had to kill Osman."

After a little pause Rader chuckled "No matter. He also was of no importance. Only a tool—but I *do* begin to believe what they say about you, Carter. I shall be *most* careful in my dealings with you."

"That goes double," I said. "Good-bye, General. Be seeing you."

"*Au revoir,* Mr. Carter. As you say, we will most certainly be seeing each other."

Eleven

The Jag was waiting for me in the Excelsior parking lot, the keys in the switch-lock. Beneath the streaky paint and the artfully battered fenders was a brand-new car—an XK-E with a top speed of 140 miles an hour. They were so new that Purg had not even had one for me to practice on; now, as I felt the raw power of the great engine, I hoped that I would never have to open it wide. Not on Swiss roads!

I had taken what I would need from Gladstone and checked the rhino-hide suitcase at the Excelsior. From now on I had to travel light. Light and fast.

I had the rest of the afternoon to kill. There was no need for evasive tactics; I didn't think that Max Rader would bother to have me followed. There was no point. Rader or his men would be at the villa sometime after dark—I couldn't imagine them coming in the day time—and they would expect to find me there, waiting. And so I would be. I was becoming more impatient with every passing minute. I wanted to face the situation, once and for all. If I had to kill Rader, and I was pretty sure I would, I wanted it over and done with. If Rader was telling the truth and Hondo was still alive, he would be no threat. And if I could get Rader's fragment of the key, so much the better. If I did not get it—and Rader would be as canny as I would myself in choosing a hiding place—then AXE would have to retire from the scene and let the diplomats take over. That would take time and matters would have to be brought into the open. The United States did not want that. Whatever there was about the golden tiger that made having it so important and urgent —and I could not even begin to guess at the real reason —I knew that the government did not want the rest of the world to know about it. That had been made clear at the briefing. Hawk and the State Department wanted a good, clean, hush-hush job, with no untidy ends. So did I. I hate loose ends.

Before leaving the hotel I had oiled and checked Wilhelmina. The stripped-down 9mm Luger was in condition GO! So was Pierre, snug in my pocket. Hugo, in my sleeve scabbard, had had a good soap-and-water and alcohol bath to cleanse the blade of every trace of Osman's blood.

As I drove along the lake toward Montreux and the good lunch I had promised myself, I wondered whether Osman was still floating at the end of his tether in the boathouse. Perhaps he had sunk by now. No matter. Probably no one would enter the boathouse for days, and no one knew of Osman's death but Mignonne Franchette and Max Rader. It would be hard to say which of them cared less.

I lunched well at a tiny Hansel and Gretel inn that was barely a stone's throw from the ancient castle of Chillon. The day had turned very fine after the brief fury of the *molan,* and I meant to enjoy it. I sipped my Clos Vougeot slowly, spinning out the peaceful moments as long as I could, and thought about the Baroness.

I was forced to admit that she affected me as no women ever had before. It was not her ardor, or her beauty, or even the air of mystery about her. Nor was it her unfortunate life that aroused my sympathy. At heart, I am not a very sympathetic man. I have always known the difference between sentiment and sentimentality; the world is a dung heap on which countries, and individuals, fight for survival. I have few tears to waste on losers.

With the complete candor possible only when one is alone, I asked myself if I was falling in love with the Baroness.

Absurd! AXE agents did not fall in love. That tender passion was for ordinary men, on the outside. For an agent it would be disaster, no less.

Yet I sat for a long time over my wine, thinking. The sun was well down in the west when I started for the villa.

The night was dark and windy, the moon hidden by a low-hanging sky with a scum of leaden clouds. The good weather had vanished with the sun; in the rising wind I could smell the moist excitement of a new storm. That was just as well. A dark night for dark deeds.

I was in the far reaches of suburban Geneva. Streets and lights were few. I was unfamiliar with the terrain and lost my way a couple of times before I found the bright colored lights of the little street carnival I had noticed the previous night. Using them as a beacon, I got my bearings and eventually found a narrow dirt road leading down to the lake across from the island and the villa. I left the Jag in a stand of silver birch where the track ended—obviously it was a lovers' rendezvous, fortunately not in use at the moment—and walked down to the lake edge. Across from me was the little island and the villa, lights glowing from every window.

I pondered for a moment when I saw all the lights. Mignonne fighting off loneliness by fighting off the darkness? Mignonne having a party, perhaps, with a few friends from the mainland? If so, that would complicate matters.

I listened for a moment to the sound of the carousel from the little carnival; then I began my search. I used my pencil-beam flashlight sparingly. For all I knew, Rader, or his men, were already on the island.

It took me five minutes to find what I was looking for —a fisherman's skiff tied to a rotting little dock at the lake's edge. As I was cheerfully stealing it I noticed that quite a few other boats were on the lake tonight. Their white, red, and green lights dotted the dark surface of the water like iridescent little gems. None were near the island. Most appeared to be heading landward as the wind continued to rise. Far down the shore I could make out the brilliant arc lights of what appeared to be a large boathouse. Most of the boats were heading in that direction. As I settled in the skiff and shoved out into the lake, I realized that Rader or his men would probably embark from that boathouse. Unless Rader's organization, with which I was becoming more and more impressed, preferred motorboats. But that I doubted. I also doubted that Rader would come to the villa in person. He was too canny for that.

I rowed around the island to approach it from the lake side. Fortunately, the oarlocks were well oiled and I made little noise. For five minutes I hovered just offshore, watching and listening, the skiff moving with the slowly increasing swell as the wind harried the lake. It was a fitful wind, backing and changing direction every minute or so, and when it was blowing from the island I could make out a faint sound of music. Mignonne Franchette playing the radio?

I beached the skiff on a muddy little beach and hauled it above the water line. Fifty feet inland the cliffs began. Using my pencil light, I finally located a rough path leading upward. Five minutes later I was in the trees behind the villa, gazing at the brilliantly lit kitchen windows.

The entire house, downstairs and up, was a blaze of light. Mignonne, if indeed she was still there, was combating the night and the storm with a vengeance. The villa was like a lighthouse in the night. I could hear the radio clearly now. It was playing a Strauss waltz.

I waited, liking the setup less and less. A most important factor was missing. No shadows moved behind the venetian blinds. No Mignonne walked before the open windows. Nothing stirred in the Villa Limbo. There were only the bright lights and the music.

I felt my skin prickle in warning. It was like watching a noisy, brilliantly lit tomb. It was entirely *too* quiet.

Yet I could not skulk in the trees forever. I moved to the left, still in the shadows, circling the villa in a crouching run. I approached each of the paths radiating from the villa with stealth, alert for danger. Nothing. No watchers, no one waiting. The island, the villa, brooded in a loud, blazing isolation that was far more menacing than shadows and silence would have been.

I completed my circle of the villa and was back at my starting point. I stopped for a moment to check the Luger in my belt, as well as Pierre and Hugo; then I ran for the kitchen door of the villa. Soon I would know.

Nothing. I pulled open a screen door and slipped into the spacious kitchen. I stopped dead, my glance riveted on the thing in the middle of the kitchen floor. A lump grew in my throat. For one of the very few times in my life, I felt pity. She had been such a cheerful, vulgar, harmless little wench!

Mignonne Franchette had died hard, clawing and scratching to preserve the life she loved so well. She lay sprawled like a rag doll in the center of the gleaming tile floor, her pretty, plump legs outflung, her chubby hands still hooked into talons. Her eyes, rolled back in her head with the whites glistening, stared with a terrible intentness at the ceiling.

I moved away from the door, still close to the wall, and stood listening. The radio was playing somewhere in the front of the house. Probably in the Comtesse's study. I remembered seeing a Telefunken there while making a cursory examination of the villa.

I crossed the kitchen swiftly and knelt beside the dead girl. No question that she was dead. Her eyes, once so warm and dark and full of desire, were now the glassy eyes of a dead animal. Again I felt stirrings of pity—and anger. Why? And who? I was sure that Mignonne had in no way been associated with Max Rader. Osman had been Rader's man, and Osman was floating dead in the little boathouse.

Who else had been on the island? Or was still on it?

I heard it. But not in time. Even my finely tuned reflexes could not save me.

What I had heard was the faintest squeak of a hinge as the pantry door opened. Something cold prodded me in the back of the neck.

Shikoku Hondo said: "Please to put up the hands, Mr. Carter."

Twelve

I knew that I was very close to death. A single breath, a trigger squeeze away from eternity. There was no margin, no leeway for even the slightest mistake. Shikoku Hondo had somehow fooled us all. Now I had to eat bitter crow and start thinking my way out of death. Think fast, KILL-MASTER!

But there was still the piece of French key. My lone ace in the hole.

I put my hands high over my head and turned around. Very slowly.

Hondo stepped back away from me. The pistol in his hand was rock-steady on my chest, though the little rat had to support himself by leaning on a chair. He looked like a drowned ghost returned from the sea to haunt mortals. He was coatless and tieless. His shirt was mud-spattered and in rags. He was shoeless. His trousers, once neatly pressed, were shapeless tubes of slime and dirt.

Playing desperately for time, I tried the bantering gambit. An Oriental would understand fear and take immediate advantage of it. A little kidding might confuse him. The Japanese were not much for gagging it up.

"You look like hell," I said. I kept my face impassive and stared at Hondo. "Your pal Rader work you over?"

Hondo gave me a look of pure hatred. His monkey face was yellow parchment stretched too tightly over the skull. His front teeth were missing.

"I know you are armed, Mr. Carter." Hondo spoke slowly, with agony twisting his flaccid lips. He sank slowly into the chair he had been leaning on. The pistol never wavered from my stomach.

"I know you are armed," Hondo repeated, "so I will not try to search you. I will not get close to you—I will give you no chance to play any of your dirty AXE tricks on me. But at the first sign—if you even begin to lower your hands—I will shoot you immediately in the most painful of places!"

For a moment the pistol moved to indicate my genitals. "I will shoot you there, Mr. Carter. I will ruin you as you have ruined me. I have been in agony—I am still in agony. It will give me the greatest pleasure to share some of it with you." Hondo moaned suddenly and bent forward to clutch at himself. But he did not take his eyes or the pistol off me.

I gave the little creep a nasty grin. "Serves you right," I said. "You were going to do a filthy thing to a sleeping girl. You got what you deserved, you dirty little bastard!"

I was gambling a lot and I knew it. I was gambling that Hondo wouldn't kill me yet. Couldn't afford to kill me yet. And I was trying to get Hondo more nervous and shook up than he already was.

Hondo's yellow claw tensed on the trigger of the pistol for a moment, then relaxed. He even managed a toothless grin through his obvious pain.

"You are a very brave man, Mr. Carter. Or a very foolish one. I am not sure which. Possibly, at this point, you even imagine that you are dictating matters?"

I stood as still as I possibly could, my hands extended to the ceiling. Any normal man would have begun to tremble, to tire, by now. I knew that I could maintain the posture for hours. I could—but I sure as hell didn't want to.

I said, "I think I *am* the boss up to a certain point. You want something I've got. Without it you're nothing,

Hondo. You're broke and sick and beat up and on the run. I doubt your passport could stand a close scrutiny —they don't give passports to ex-cons, not even in your country. Especially not to war criminals.

"Max Rader's got no use for you now. I suppose you know he meant to kill you? He told me so himself."

Hondo's little eyes glistened. "I know. General Rader is a Prussian—and something of a fool. But I fooled him —I escaped his dungeon."

I pretended admiration, being careful not to overdo it. By now I was sure that Hondo did not know that Rader's men were coming to the villa tonight. For once I was anxious to leap from the frying pan into the fire. By a strange quirk of fate, my enemies might be the ones to save me. But it was not going to be easy to keep Hondo talking. He was near death himself and he would not care who he took with him.

I tried to con him along. "I don't see how you got away from Rader. He told me he had you wrapped up good and tight."

Hondo bared his gums in a bitter smile. "We Orientals have a manner of looking at things—it is to look for the obvious. The obvious that is always overlooked by you of the West. There was an air vent in my dungeon, from long ago when the moat was deeper and the water not so high. Now the water in the moat is higher and the end of the vent is under water. The fools did not stop to think that a little man can squeeze through a small space. And that a man can hold his breath and swim. I did so. I got out. I thought you would be here because Rader was having the girl watched. He knows about this place—he has known for years that the girl comes here. He has had a man planted here to watch her."

I immediately picked up and stored the key words: Moat—dungeon—air vent. Max Rader must be holed up in some sort of castle! But that didn't narrow it down as much as I had hoped. There were a lot of old castles around this part of the world.

"Rader is going to kill the girl, isn't he?"

Hondo nodded. "When he is ready. She has seen his new face. Anyway, she is his enemy and hates him. She will never give up. He must kill her."

I was puzzled. "But you—you've seen his new face too. Don't you know what that means?"

To my surprise, Hondo shook his head. The pistol kept its deadly, unwinking vigil on my abdomen.

"I have *not* seen his new face," Hondo said. "Always he has worn a mask when we meet and talk. It is best. I do not want to know what he looks like. As long as I do not know that he will not think he has to kill me!"

"He was going to kill you anyway," I taunted. "He told me. I advised him to sink you very deep in the lake, Hondo. To put a lot of iron on you."

Hondo winced in pain. He gave a little groan. He said, "You crazy Americans have a saying—to count the chickens before they are hatched. It is that way with Rader—and you. It is true that without my half of the key I have no face. I am nothing. But once I have it back, the matter will be different. Rader will need me again. We will obtain the tiger and separate and that will be the end of it. But now no more talking, Carter. I am weary and sick. Where is my half of the French key?"

"Where you will never find it," I said coolly. "Why don't you stop bluffing, Hondo? You know you can't afford to kill me. And *I* know it. You can't scare me, either, and that leaves you nowhere. You had better put that gun down and be sensible. Maybe we can work something out. You want to get even with Rader, don't you?" It was a pretty obvious gambit and I hadn't much hope it would work. Still, it was a chance.

It didn't come off.

Hondo's skull-face tightened. He shoved the pistol at me to emphasize his words. "You are playing for time,

Carter. I do not understand why. Nothing can help you here. And my patience is wearing thin. You had better tell me where the key is, while you are still able to speak normally. Soon you will be screaming. You will be begging for death. And I, Mr. Carter, will not give you death. It will seem the most precious thing in the world—death! But you will not get it—not until you tell me where the key is! Not until I check and see that you have not lied. Then, if my mood is kindly, Carter, I may give you death!"

My arms were beginning to feel the strain a bit now. Just a bit. But I kept them steady above my head, unwavering, giving Hondo no excuse to shoot. His last words sent a little chill creeping through me. The little bastard seemed cocksure of himself. I remembered what I had learned about Hondo during my briefings, and from Hawk. The little crud had liked to chop off the heads of captured GIs. And there was Mignonne Franchette, sprawled on the kitchen floor, not six feet away. I glanced at the body. Maybe I could keep Hondo talking a few seconds longer.

I nodded at the dead girl. "Did you have to kill her? She was just a harmless little peasant girl. She wasn't in on this."

Hondo's unblinking stare did not leave me. He did not even glance at the body. "She was in the way," he said. "She was afraid of me and she screamed. And she was strong—it took all my power to strangle her. If I had let her go she would have brought the police. So what matter? She is nothing!"

Hondo groaned as he pulled himself up from the chair. "But she was lucky, Carter. She died quickly. More than you will do unless you tell me where the key is. Now! Immediately! And do not bother to lie, because we will go together to find it. You will hand it to me."

I allowed an expression of fear and despair to show on my face. "And if I do that?"

Hondo nodded slowly. "I will kill you, of course. But I will kill you with mercy. A bullet in the brain."

"Doesn't sound like much of a bargain," I said. "And if I don't?"

Hondo's laugh was weak but vicious. "You will wish you had, I can promise. And you will, in the end. Now, Mr. Carter—no more talk. If you say one more word I am going to shoot you in a most painful place." Again Hondo pointed to my groin.

"I am going to count to ten," he went on. "Slowly I will count to ten. If you do not tell me where the key is—and no lies—I will shoot you there. You will not die of it. Not for hours. While you are groveling and screaming on the floor I will begin the little game I have in mind. In my country it is called the Death of a Thousand Cuts!"

Hondo's expression was pure evil mixed with sadistic anticipation. "I will have to hurry it a bit, I am afraid. There is not all the time I would like. I will have to make it the death of a hundred cuts—but that will be enough, I am sure. I am sure *you* will find it quite enough!"

Hondo backed away from me, cautiously, never taking his eyes off me. He reached behind him, into the drawer of a cabinet, and took out a long, shiny butcher's knife. Light glinted from the blade as he waved it in my face. "A hundred cuts," he said. "A little of you at a time, Mr. Carter. An inch of flesh here, an inch there. An ear. Part of a nose. A slice of lip. How much of you will be left before you talk, Mr. Carter?"

My ears were much sharper than Hondo's. I heard them, someone, stealthily approaching the back door. Rader's men. Maybe they would help me out of this, maybe not. No way of knowing if I would be better off—or worse. But at least it was a reprieve. And I still had my weapons. Now I might have a chance to use them.

To distract Hondo for the remaining seconds, I said: "I sure made a mistake when I didn't kill you. I thought

I had. How *did* you miss being killed, anyway? That was a long fall."

Hondo smirked. "I am fortunate. I fell into a pile of boxes and trash that broke my fall. Rader's men found me and took me back to the castle. Now, Mr. Carter— one—two—thr——"

There came a burst of fire from the door. Hondo screamed and spun around, flinging his pistol across the room. He slid down to the shiny kitchen floor, his legs kicking and beating about, his skinny hands tearing at the bloody holes in his chest as though he could tear out the bullets that were killing him.

The man in the Trilby hat fired three more times at Hondo. Pointblank into the little bastard's body. Hondo arched once and blood spewed from his toothless mouth. Then he moaned and slobbered a word in his native language. Then nothing. Colonel Shikoku Hondo was with his ancestors.

Thirteen

"Hold your fire!"

My voice crackled with authority. With lightning swiftness I produced both Wilhelmina and Pierre. I held the Luger in my right hand, the muzzle slightly depressed. I opened my left palm to show them the deadly little gas bomb.

"Rader doesn't want me dead," I said rapidly. "I don't want to kill you. Even if you get me, I'll drop this bomb as I fall. You'll be dead before you can take a step. So everyone hold it!"

I faced them across the contorted body of Hondo. Trilby hat and two men behind him in the kitchen door. Which way would the ball bounce?

The man in the Trilby hat slowly allowed his pistol to sink to the floor. He was wearing a trench coat now instead of the leather windbreaker. "*Ja,* iss better," he said, in a thick German accent. "*Jawohl.* Hans—Pieter! You hear?"

Two soft *ja*s from his companions. They took their hands out of their pockets and stepped into the kitchen. I motioned to chairs around the kitchen table. I picked up the chair on which Hondo had leaned and retreated to a corner. Very slowly I put Wilhelmina on the floor. But I kept the little gas bomb in my left hand, where the men could see it.

"Now let's all have a nice little chat," I said. "Make yourselves comfortable, gentlemen. Sorry I can't offer you any refreshment, but things have been just a little hectic around here. In any case, as you can see, our maid has had a sort of fatal accident." I nodded toward the body of Mignonne Franchette.

The man in the Trilby hat stared at the dead woman with little hard, bright-blue eyes. He looked at me. "Who did?"

I pointed to Hondo's body. "Your little pal there."

Trilby hat spat on the shiny kitchen floor. *"Schwein."*

I nodded. "I agree." To me, the man in the Trilby hat, with his flattened nostrils and flabby lips, looked a little like a pig himself. I thought it better not to bring up the matter at the moment. I crossed my legs and allowed myself to relax a bit, hoping they would take a hint and do the same.

"I'd like a cigarette," I told them. "Can I put my hand in my pocket without starting fireworks?"

Trilby hat regarded me for a moment. It was evident that he did not dig this crazy *Amerikaner* in the least. But he said, "Iss okay. Ve all smoke, *ja.*"

He put his pistol carefully on the table, the muzzle pointing toward me, and took a pack of cigarettes from his pocket. His two companions did the same, their eyes never leaving me. They were both stocky men in raincoats and soft felt hats. I thought I recognized them as the men who had been watching outside the Hotel Lux. Tweedledum and Tweedledee. Bully-boy types. Hired muscle. Their type was a dime a dozen.

I exhaled a cloud of blue smoke at the ceiling. I leaned forward. "Now," I said. "Let's get down to the real business, shall we? I take it that Rader couldn't come in person?"

Trilby hat gave me a hard blue stare. "Ze General iss send us to bring you to ze *schloss.* You vill come, please, und bring *mit* you vat ze General vants! *Ja?*"

"Nein!" I stared back at the man. "I will come to the castle when I am ready, not before! That will be soon,

but I will not go with you. I have things to do here first." I pointed at the body of Mignonne. "I liked that one. You understand? She and I were lovers. I want to take care of her body decently. And I must clean up the place—I don't want to leave anything for the police to find."

Trilby hat gave me a stubborn stare. "Ve haff our orders! Ve bring you und ze property of ze General!"

I chuckled. "That's pretty rich—the property of the General! I'm sorry, friends, but we'll have to do it my way. You just go back and tell the General that I'll be along shortly. I'll give him a call first, so he can be prepared. You have a phone at this castle?"

The man nodded. "*Ja.* Iss phone. But better you come mit us now, I think—"

"I don't," I said abruptly. I tossed Pierre into the air about a foot and caught the little bomb as it came down. Three pairs of eyes swiveled to follow the motion. "I'm a pretty good juggler," I said. "But if you guys keep arguing, I just might get careless. None of us wants that, I'm sure. So we play it my way, huh?"

Trilby surrendered with ill grace. "*Ja.* Ve do it your vay. But you remember ve haff ze girl! Und you vill bring no veapon! Ve vill search you before you are allowed to enter ze *schloss*. Most thorough ve vill search —mit all your clothes taken off! You understand, *nein?*"

I grinned at them. "*Ja.* I understand. No veapons! So suppose you take off now and tell Rader, tell the General, that I'll be there soon. I accept his kind invitation to the ball. Tell him I like Strauss waltzes. Now, just write down the phone number and tell me how to get there. Then take off. And take that carrion with you." I pointed to the body of Hondo. "Sink it deep," I advised. "We don't want him coming back again, do we?"

Trilby grunted an order at his companions. They walked around me, careful not to get in the line of fire, and each seized a foot of the dead man. They dragged him out the back door. He had bled profusely and now left a great wide smear of blood across the kitchen floor.

Trilby took a notebook from his pocket and scribbled in it. He tore out the page and fluttered it across at me. "Iss phone. *Schloss* iss on ze Rhône—ze river! Iss last place on ze Avenue Brisson. You know?"

I knew I could find the castle without difficulty. Part of my briefing for this job had been an intensive study of area maps. I nodded. "I'll be there. West of the city, isn't it? About where the Rhône comes into the town?"

"*Ja.*"

Trilby, his eyes steady on mine, picked up his pistol and carefully stowed it away in a shoulder clip. "You come soon," he said. "Ze General iss not a patient man. *Und* he is not like ze girl. You try tricks somesing bad happen to her." His fatty lips parted to show brown-stained teeth in a cruel grin. "Somesing bad happen to you too—if you try tricks. Iss old *schloss,* you understand? Ve have nice torture chamber!"

"How charming!" I said coldly. "Screams in the night, eh? The rack and the iron lady and the hot irons? The boot?"

Trilby nodded. He grinned again. "*Ja, ja!* Ve haff all. Iss in old part of *schloss.* Not use for a long time. But ve keep ze machinery oiled, *nein?*"

"I'll just bet you do."

Trilby nodded again and started for the door, walking sideways, always facing me. "Iss okay zen. You come soon. You bring vat ze General vants. *Und* no monkey-shining, *nein?* Vill be very bad for ze girl *und* you if you try tricks."

I stood up, smiling blandly. "I promise. All I want is to get the girl back safely." I crossed my fingers. "I promise—nary a monkeyshining."

"*Ja.* I see you." Trilby hat backed out the door and was gone.

I glanced at my watch. A quarter of ten. There was a

lot to do and not much time to do it. Working fast, I found a bucket and mop and swabbed up Hondo's blood.

I carried the body of Mignonne Franchette up to my suite and put her on the bed. Before I put a sheet over her I stood for a moment gazing down. Poor little thing. She had been so damned full of life—lust if you pleased—and wanted only to enjoy herself. Now she ended like this. I sighed and pulled the sheet over her face. I am not much given to emotion, yet the injury and death of innocent bystanders always pains me. But Hondo had paid. Now to get on with it. Time was slipping away. If my steadily burgeoning plan was to work, I must act quickly.

You could never foresee everything and I had not counted on the weather turning sour again. I went to Osman's room and found a tent-sized black rubber poncho. Good. It would keep me reasonably dry and help cloak me in the darkness.

I took a large waterproof pouch from my pocket. In it I placed the Luger, the gas bomb, and the little stiletto. I tied up the package securely and gave it a final pat. "Have to part with you for a little, old friends," I murmured. I didn't like doing it, but there seemed no other way. For once I would have to break my own rule and go up against the enemy without a weapon. I grinned. No veapons, Trilby had said. And I had agreed. But I hadn't said for how long.

I tucked the pouch containing Wilhemina, Pierre, and Hugo into my belt. I took a large supply of towels from one of the bathrooms. I slid Osman's poncho over my head. I turned off every light in the villa, then went to stand on one of the iron balconies. It was raining hard now, and the wind was gaining force. The night was dungeon-dark. Wind hurled gusts of cold rain into my face. I stood in the weeping, susurrant blackness and listened. Faintly, over the moan of the wind, I heard the steady chug-chugging of an outboard motor. Trilby and his boys departing. I smiled. I hoped they had weighted Hondo well.

An hour later I wheeled the Jaguar off the desolate Avenue Brisson into a narrow lane that ran behind the Schloss Brunhild. I had been furnished with an excellent large-scale ordnance map by Special Effects and Editing. It was paying off.

I drove with the lights off now, feeling my way along the muddy, rutted lane. It ended in a little copse of black, wind-tossed trees. I cut the engine and listened to the rain beat on the canvas top of the roadster. The night was turning more foul by the second—and that suited me fine.

I took a small tin from my jacket and proceeded to black my face with the greaseless preparation, which would come off swiftly and easily. I risked a single glance in the rearview mirror, using my pencil-beam flash. My eyes glinted fiercely back at me. Enough to scare even me, I thought, as I flicked off the light. I looked like a demon from the black pits of hell.

I stripped rapidly, squirming and twisting in the little car. Finally I was down to a pair of black shorts. I smeared the rest of my body with the paste.

I tucked the waterproof pouch containing my weapons into my trunks and shrugged into Osman's huge poncho. I was nearly ready now. I stepped out into the gale-swept night and closed the car door softly. The rain beat down on me with the fury of surf.

I went to the rear of the Jag and opened the trunk and took out a small entrenching tool. I hoped I wouldn't need it—but you never knew. Then I started for the Schloss Brunhild, crouching in the storm. Waiting.

The going was rough. It was treacherous underfoot. I fell several times, cursing softly. I blundered through dense undergrowth. Brambles clawed at the black poncho. Finally I came to what I had feared—a high wire fence. Just beyond it was the old part of the *schloss*, a ruined medieval pile, turreted and towered and with old battle-

ments pierced for arrow fire. Around it a moat glinted
black and inky, sluggish and evil-looking in an occasional
flash of lightning.

I kept well back from the fence as I considered it.
Possibly it was electrified, but I didn't think so. That
could cause trouble, an accident, and the last thing Max
Rader wanted was to call attention to himself.

No—it wouldn't be electrified. But just as certainly there
would be some sort of warning system. Probably when
you touched the fence a bell would sound in the inhabited
part of the *schloss*.

I went cautiously to work with the entrenching tool.
When you couldn't go over, you went under!

In ten minutes I had a trench deep enough to allow
me to wriggle under the fence without touching it. Rain
had softened the ground, for which I was grateful.

I left the entrenching tool by the fence, making a
mental note to be sure to collect it when I left. I went to
the edge of the moat. The water lapped coldly at my
feet. I was pulling the poncho over my head when I
heard it—a savage snarl in the darkness!

The Doberman came out of nowhere, a black lance of
slavering fury. I was entangled in the poncho, and it was
the heavy rubber that saved my throat. I went down
under the onslaught, writhing beneath eighty pounds of
kill-crazy dog.

For a moment cold fear invaded me. I had been caught
off-guard and weaponless. The Luger, the gas bomb, the
stiletto—they were all in the envelope in my belt. There
was no time—and if the dog barked I was finished.

But the Doberman did not bark. It was content with
the feral snarls welling from its deep throat. It disentangled
the gleaming fangs from the poncho and came at me
again, long white teeth flashing. I tossed the poncho
aside and fell sideways, rolling with the creature as it
struck me a second time.

I had to kill the dog with my bare hands. I got one

hand around the Doberman's sleek throat, my fingers digging deep into the mass of muscle and sinew. I held the slavering beast away from me until I could bring my other hand to bear. The strain was inhuman, tremendous, nearly impossible, even for me. The Doberman was a writhing, straining, furious eighty pounds of sleek-pelted dynamite.

I stood up, holding the dog at arm's length, slowly throttling the life out of the splendid animal. With regret. The dog was another innocent bystander. It was only doing its job. What men had trained it to do.

The beast died hard. It was a full three minutes before it quivered for the last time. I dropped the warm carcass and stood breathing heavily. Damn! I should have foreseen the possibility of dogs. Max Rader didn't miss a trick.

For another minute I waited and listened. Nothing but the moan of wind and the steady slanting beat of rain. I picked up the dead Doberman and carried it into the black waters of the moat. It would be found eventually, but by that time it wouldn't matter.

I let the dog drift away and got my bearings. I was just opposite the old part of the *schloss*. The battlements brooded over me, crumbling and covered with the slime and weed of centuries. Somewhere in that moldering pile of rock, I knew, was the dungeon where Hondo had been kept. From which he had managed to escape. And if Hondo had gotten out, surely KILLMASTER could get in! And out!

I began to circle the *schloss,* using a noiseless breast stroke, only my nostrils above water. A good "recon" was always in order.

I moved slowly and silently through the murky water. At places the banks of the old moat had given away and the water formed a darkling tarn. I kept close in under the walls of the *schloss.*

I rounded a bend in the moat and saw the new part of

the *schloss*. It seemed a fairly recent addition. Not more than a hundred years old. Four stories high, it was built of whitish stone, rain-dark now, and resembled a squat, round tower. Lights gleamed cheerfully from windows here and there.

I could not quite believe what I saw next. A drawbridge. A real drawbridge. It was up, cutting off the modern driveway that led into it from the Avenue Brisson. There's probably a portcullis, too, I thought wryly. Rader *doesn't* overlook much.

I heard a man cough and saw the tiny spark of a cigarette in the gloom near the *schloss* side of the raised drawbridge. A guard. Nothing surprising there. Of course there would be a guard. They were expecting company, remember? Me.

Well, just be patient, fella. I'll be there.

I filled my lungs and submerged. I was under for three minutes, swimming strongly and silently, and when I surfaced I was at the rear of the *schloss*. I continued around until I was back at my starting point. Somewhere in this slimy stone, beneath the water line, was the old air vent from which Hondo had escaped.

I dove and began to search. It took me five minutes to find it. A round tube in the stone from which the ancient iron grille had rusted away. It was going to be a narrow squeeze for someone my size. For Hondo it must have been easy.

I surfaced and thought it over for a moment. I knew the risks. I didn't really know what was in that pipe. Part of it was underwater. It must rise inside the *schloss*, then descend again to the dungeons. But if I got stuck in there! Even my lungs were only good for four minutes. It would be a most unpleasant death—a terrifying death.

I took ten deep breaths to make ready. I sucked the rain-swept air down to the very bottom of my lungs. I did not allow myself to think that this air might be the very last I would ever breathe. The thing had to be done

—this way. Max Rader was in there. The Baroness von Stadt was in there. I had told Hawk that I would get her out and this I must do. Most important of all—the other half of the French key was in there.

I took a final breath, checked to see that my three weapons were secure in their pouch, and went under.

Fourteen

On the stroke of midnight I braked the Jag to a stop before the raised drawbridge of the Schloss Brunhild. The storm was steadily increasing in fury. The windshield wipers could hardly handle the blasting rain. I tooted the horn, giving the signal agreed on when I had phoned Max Rader. Three shorts — two longs—three shorts.

Lights went on in a stone guardhouse across the moat. The bridge began to clank and rumble down, controlled by a modern windlass. All the conveniences of the modern home, I thought cynically. Even a built-in torture chamber!

While I waited for the bridge to settle into place I glanced at myself in the rearview mirror. Every hair was in place. I had taken a bath in the rain after emerging from the dungeons—it paid to look your best when you went calling.

The drawbridge lurched into place with a final clank. A man in a slicker and sodden hat signaled me with a flashlight. I drove the Jag into the *schloss*. Behind me I heard the rumble of the bridge starting up again. The mouse was in the trap. The fly was in the web.

I yawned. Someone was in for a fooling, and I didn't think it would be KILLMASTER. But then you never knew, did you? Every trail had a turning. Luck had to run out sometime. I yawned again, a deliberate device to ease the tension that was building inside me. My nerves were as taut as violin strings. This was it. The payoff.

I was signaled to a halt in a smallish inner courtyard. A man pulled the car door open. It was my old friend, the man in the Trilby hat. "Out," came the command. "Out mit hands up, please. No tricks."

"Sure," I said easily. "I promised, didn't I? No monkeyshining." I got out of the car and stood in the rain with my hands over my head. Trilby patted me up and down. It was a cursory search and I understood that it was only a preliminary. Behind Trilby, to one side, another man was covering me with a submachine gun.

I stood perfectly still. My eyes roamed the shadowy, rain-swept courtyard, taking in everything. I counted six of them, two with machine guns, the rest with handguns. With Trilby, that made seven. And probably more inside. Pretty long odds. Rader sported an elaborate organization. Must cost a fortune, too. I sighed inwardly. Not to worry. If my plan came off, the odds would even out. If not, well, maybe Hawk would send flowers.

Trilby gave me a little shove. "Forvard!" He and a man with a machine gun fell in behind me. They ushered me into a barren little room off the main entrance to the *schloss*. There was nothing in the room but a table and a couple of chairs. The single overhead bulb was a 250-watter, filling the tiny space with blinding white light.

Trilby and the machine gunner remained at the door. Trilby leered at me. "You, *Amerikaner,* are either a fool or crazy in ze head. Take off ze clothes, please. All ze clothes!"

"Maybe I'm both," I said mildly. "Did I hear you right? You want me to undress?"

"Ja! Und hurry. Ve vaste time. Ze General iss vaiting."

"Well—if I must." I began to strip.

There followed the most intensive and thorough search I had ever undergone. Trilby knew his business. My clothes were turned inside out. Every possible place was searched, even the secret crevices of my body. This was all to the good. I had counted on just this. It was an integral part of my plan. I wanted Max Rader relaxed, at his ease and off-guard.

"Hey," I told Trilby, "that tickles! Cut it out, will you!"

Trilby finished his work and stepped back. The puzzled expression in his hard blue eyes said that he would never, never, understand the crazy Yanks. Joking at a time like this! He barked an order at the machine gunner and flung my clothes at me. I began to dress. I put on a pair of white shorts. I had thrown the black trunks away on my way back to the car. I wanted no questions. Even a hint of suspicion was too much.

"Come," said Trilby. He led the way and I followed. The gunner brought up the rear, six paces behind.

We paraded down a long, dimly lit hall with a parquet floor. Halfway down, a wide stairway curved up to a shadowy gallery overlooking the hall.

The hall ended at a pair of tall double doors. Trilby rapped sharply on the doors and waited, never taking his eyes off me. The machine gunner kept his distance, his ugly weapon trained on my torso.

The door was opened by another guard. He stood aside to let me pass. Trilby gave me an ugly grin as he turned away. "Goot luck," he said.

I ignored him. I was staring across the great room to the man behind the massive desk. The man stood up and pointed to a chair before the desk. "Welcome, Mr. Carter. At long last we meet. Come and sit down."

The guard behind me gave me a little push, an urging that I did not need. I wanted to get it over with now as fast as possible. We were right down to the nub. No possible margin for error remained. I walked toward the desk and the man behind it. As I walked my mind collected facts and stored them.

The psychological setup was skillful. There was only one bright light in the room, and it was so arranged that it would shine full in my face. My chair was placed to seat me lower than the man at the desk, whose face would be in shadow.

All very skillful, I admitted. But it wasn't going to do Rader much good.

I halted beside the indicated chair. Max Rader, former general in the *Schutzstaffel,* was still standing by his desk. Now he came a part way around it, into the edge of brightness. I could see him quite plainly.

Rader motioned to the chair with a lean, well-cared-for hand. "Please sit down. I will not offer to shake hands, Mr. Carter. I think we both agree that such a gesture would be hypocrisy. We are both very practical men, both here for a very practical purpose. Let us get on with it—but first, if you like, a drink? A cigar?"

"No thanks." I sank into the chair, keeping my eyes on Rader. I was aware of a feeling of surprise without knowing exactly why. This was a handsome man. Tall, lean, with a good military carriage. If he was wearing a corset, in the Prussian manner, it did not show. The face was good, too. A smooth hawk's face under a thick crop of short, iron-gray hair. The nose jutted determinedly over a thin but not unpleasing mouth. I chalked one up for the plastic surgeon who had worked on Rader. This was a far cry from the ratlike face I had studied in an old photo of Rader.

I could hear sounds around me now. Faint stirrings in the outer shadows of the huge room. We were not alone, of course. My eyes were becoming accustomed to the interplay of light and shadow. To keep Rader off balance a moment longer, I said: "I congratulate you. They did a marvelous job on your face. But why didn't they take off the dueling scar?"

Rader, who was still standing near the end of the big desk, checked an involuntary movement of his hand to the scar. It was a long, puckered welt, a living scimitar slashing from the corner of his left eye down to his mouth.

Rader dropped his hand and stared at me for a moment

before he answered. "It is a badge of honor, Mr. Carter. Of courage, if you like. One does not throw away such things. But let us not talk about me—let us talk about you. You and the pretty Baroness and the French key. You have it with you?"

I shook my head. Here was where the stuff hit the fan.

"No," I said. "I didn't bring it."

Someone gasped in the shadows just outside the ring of light. I peered in the direction of the sound. I saw her. The Baroness. She was sitting there in a chair, apparently unbound, staring at me with her great gray eyes. She was still wearing the gray slacks and the green sweater. Even in the poor light I could see that she was very pale.

"Oh, Nicky," she said. "Oh, Nicky—you should have brought it. We are beaten, Nicky. And I—I am afraid!"

She sounded afraid. Afraid and bewildered and defeated.

I leaned forward in my chair. I grinned encouragement at her. "Take it easy, kid. Keep your chin up. We're not licked yet."

"Mr. Carter!"

Max Rader held up a slim hand, now on the verge of crooking into a talon. The oil of courtesy left his voice. It now had the harsh arrogance I had heard on the phone.

"Are you telling me, Mr. Carter, that you did *not* bring the key? I find that hard to believe, sir. Surely you realize your position!" There was a trace of malignancy in Rader's face now—the edge of the hatchet was showing.

I crossed my legs. I adjusted a sock leisurely. "Yes," I admitted. "I am telling you I did not bring the French key. I lied so I could get in here. I had to talk to you, Rader. Make you see your position. And mine. Because I think I'm calling the shots. You've got to have that key and I've got it."

Max Rader regarded me for a moment. He had regained his icy composure. He made a little steeple with his thin fingers. I noticed, for the first time, that the man was wearing evening clothes. A dinner jacket. On his left breast a decoration glittered—the Iron Cross, first class.

Rader said: "It is true that you have the key, Mr. Carter. But on the other hand—I most certainly have you."

"You seem to know a lot about me," I said. "Who I am—all that. How do you know I haven't got the joint ringed with my friends? With agents? Maybe the Swiss police?"

Rader shook his head. "I think not. You are as off limits in this country as I am. The Swiss do not like their country used as a battleground. If you are caught, your country will disown you. Officially, at least. I know a little of such matters. As an officer of the SS I worked in close liaison with our security police, the *Sicherheitsdienst*. No, Mr. Carter. You are quite alone. And certainly in no position to bargain."

I shrugged. "Okay. I'll admit that I'm alone. But I *am* in a position to bargain." I jerked my head upward, toward the dark galleries surrounding the room. "You have armed men up there?"

As if in answer to my query, someone coughed on the gallery, and there was a scraping of feet on bare flooring.

Rader inclined his head. "Of course. You are being covered by a machine gun at this very moment. Perhaps it is not necessary—after all, you were thoroughly searched—"

"I sure was," I interrupted. "I couldn't possibly have a weapon on me. Doesn't that make you think a little, Rader? Would I walk into a trap like this if I didn't think—didn't *know*—I held the upper hand? And I'll tell you why I hold it, Rader." I leaned forward to stare hard at the man behind the desk. I could hear the nervous breathing of the Baroness in the shadows, but I ignored her. It was hard on her, yes, but it had to be played this way.

"I'll tell you," I repeated. "Because you can't afford to

kill me. And I won't let you torture me, Rader. I can lick any four men you've got in the place without guns. I won't let you take me alive. I'll make you kill me! And if things should get too tough I've got a cyanide pill I can take before your goons could possibly stop me."

"You couldn't have," rasped Rader. "My men searched—"

"For weapons," I said with a grin. I went on to compound the lie. "For weapons, yes. But a pill is a tiny thing. Hard to find even for experts. Your pal Goering did it, remember? So did I. But I hope I don't have to use it. That's up to you, Rader. I just want to be sure you understand. I'm in the driver's seat—not you."

It was a desperate bluff. I sat and waited to see if it would come off.

For the next few moments I thought it was going to work. Rader was staring at me silently, caressing his lean chin with his fingers. Finally: "Supposing—just supposing, Mr. Carter—that I agree with what you say. What do you propose?"

I smiled. "I propose that we cut out all this melodramatic nonsense." I nodded toward the Baroness, who was watching with fascination from her chair. "Let her go. Call off your bully boys. Then you and I, Rader, will go to the bank of Paul Chardet et Fils first thing in the morning and get the gold tiger. After I retrieve my half of the key, of course."

Rader permitted himself a thin smile. *"Your* half, Mr. Carter?"

I nodded. "I consider it so. Hondo is dead. Or didn't your men tell you?"

Rader nodded. "They told me. Good riddance. If it had not been for Hondo's suspicions I would not be in this stalemate. But he would not trust me. Would not listen. He insisted on going in person to the Hotel Lux and—" Rader broke off. "But I wander. Pray continue, Mr. Carter, with this ridiculous proposal of yours. I find such impudence almost refreshing. What happens after we get to the bank? Just the two of us?"

"Simple," I said. "I told you. You get the tiger and a good head start. I get the rest of the loot in the vault. There must be millions. Enough to save my face with my boss. As I told you on the phone, Rader, I've got to come up with something. If I can't give them the tiger I'll have to give them something else. Actually, by rigging the story a little, I can make it look pretty good. You know how Americans are about the value of human life. I think I can squeeze through on that angle—the only way I could save my life, and that of the Baroness von Stadt, was to give you the tiger. They just might buy it. Of course, they'll be after you again—" I shrugged. "That's your lookout!"

Max Rader made another little steeple with his fingers. He peered over it for a long time at me. It was fifty-fifty now—might go either way.

It went against me.

Rader said: "You are really amazing, Mr. Carter, to think I would fall for such a childish trick. You are forgetting something—I also have the Baroness!"

So it had failed. I segued rapidly into another role. "What about the Baroness?" I let a bored indifference seep into my voice. "She's not really important, Rader. She was only working with me—to identify you. But none of that is important now."

Rader's laugh was nasty. "On the contrary, it is very important. Most important! I agree that I cannot coerce you by conventional means. I give you that. Certainly I do not want to kill you. But the Baroness is another matter—I can make you watch while she is tortured, Mr. Carter. And you Americans are not very good at that."

The Baroness' gasp was audible throughout the large chamber. "No! Please no! I couldn't stand—don't let him, Nicky!"

KILLMASTER played another trump. I was getting

low on trumps now. I had one more in reserve. The big one. But this was not the time or place to play it.

I said: "I'm sorry, honey. I didn't mean to get you into this. But I guess I was wrong—I thought Rader was a reasonable man, a civilized man. I still think so. He's bluffing."

Max Rader was watching me closely. "So you think I am bluffing? How about you? Are you pretending that you do not *care* if the Baroness is tortured?"

I pretended indignation. "Of course I care. Do you think I'm an animal? I would hate to see her tortured. But—"

Rader leaned over the desk. "But?"

I sank back. I shrugged, trying to look as hangdog as possible. "I'm not a professional hero," I blurted. "I'm trying to do a job, any way I can. Torturing the Baroness won't get you the key, Rader. I beg you not to do it. But if you do, I'll still have the upper hand. You'll be torturing her for nothing! The only way you'll get that tiger is by agreeing to my plan."

A gasp of disbelief came from the Baroness. "Nicky— you would let them? Oh, my God!"

I did not meet her eyes. "I'm sorry, honey, I really am. But there's nothing I can do."

Rader's voice was soft and dry. It reminded me of a snake slithering through dry leaves.

"Her flesh is very white and lovely," Rader said. "The thought of it being torn by red-hot pincers is not a pretty one."

I stared at him boldly. "You won't do it. You're bluffing, Rader!"

Rader leaned back in his chair. He peered at me over the steepled fingers. He hooded his eyes like a falcon. "*You're* bluffing, Carter. You are doing a very good job of it, too. But not good enough. I once lived in Brooklyn. A long time ago. One of the things I learned in your country was to play poker. I am going to call your bluff,

Mr. Carter. We shall see, very soon we shall see, how much of the Baroness' pain *you* can bear!"

Rader swiveled in his chair and barked an order in German. Men came out of the shadows and surrounded me. The Baroness was jerked roughly to her feet.

"Take them to the dungeons in the old *schloss*," Rader commanded. His eyes glinted at me. "We shall see who bluffs!"

Fifteen

The little chamber, buried deep in the old *schloss*, reeked of evil and pain. Dim electric bulbs set in ancient iron sconces did nothing to dispel the illusion. Rader and his men did not wear black hoods and masks, but the effect was the same. They were killers, torturers, executioners. Here to do a job.

I won't say I wasn't worried, but I was not worried enough to abandon my plan to do a little executing of my own. My gamble had come off. Rader had taken the bait. We were in the torture chamber.

I had been here before.

There was a rusting suit of armor near the door. In one of the iron gauntlets was tucked—Pierre! In the other —Hugo! Faithful friends waiting.

But it was Wilhelmina, the deadly 9mm Luger, on which I was counting the most. The Luger was taped to the underside of the rack on which they were now stretching the Baroness von Stadt.

I made a fast survey of the place. It was small, dark, the ancient walls leaking moisture. The door behind me was wooden, but it was solid and heavy, with a massive iron bar on the outside.

Rader was standing beside me. Now he said, "Do you still think I'm bluffing?"

I gulped. Part of my act. I hoped I looked pale and sick. But I said, "Yes. I do. You won't go through with it."

Rader made a sign. One of the men at the rack started to tug off the Baroness' sweater. Her feet were already anchored to the rack. Her legs were spread-eagled, but her arms were still free. She fought the men, uttering little screams mixed with the curses she knew so well.

"Nicky! Please, for God's sake, Nicky! Don't let them —don't let them!"

I felt Rader's eyes on me. I kept my face screwed into an expression of anguish, of slowly growing doubt. I fumbled for a handkerchief and wiped my brow.

They had her green sweater off now. One of the men ripped at a white bra. The firm, pale breasts tumbled in the dim light like ripe fruits. The Baroness screamed and tried to cover herself, but they seized her arms and forced her down on the rack. In a moment her wrists were bound to the pulling cords. Likewise her ankles. In the old days these expert executioners would have wasted no time in slowly tearing her apart.

The two men beside the Baroness were staring at her naked flesh. Rader snapped an order. "Prepare the irons, you fools. We are not here for a peep show for your amusement!" One of the men turned to where an iron was heating in a charcoal brazier. He worked a bellows and the charcoal glowed a fiery red.

I took a last look around. I would be up against Rader —I did not think the man was armed—and four others: the two men at the rack and two more behind me, between me and the door. One of these men had a machine gun.

The man at the brazier lifted a nasty-looking pair of iron pincers from the coals. They were white-hot. They smoked and gave off a sickening odor. For a moment I imagined I could hear the cries of agony that must have filled this charnel pit in past centuries. The sweating walls seemed to rush in, to be crushing me.

At my side, Max Rader said, "Beautiful, aren't they?" He was staring at the Baroness, now naked from the waist up. "It seems a pity to spoil them." He looked at me. "There is still time, you know. This thing will be on your head, Carter. Can you really bear to watch her being mutilated?"

It was time. I dabbed at my brow again with the handkerchief. I choked. I turned to Rader. "Wait! Y— you win! I can't let you do it!"

Max Rader smiled thinly. "Now you are being sensible." He flipped a hand at the two men near the rack. "Let her go."

I pushed past Rader, scowling. "Keep away from her, you bastards! You've done enough. I'll take care of her."

Rader smiled tolerantly and nodded to his men. "It's all right." Sarcasm edged his voice. "We will give the lovers a couple of minutes—then we get down to business!"

I bent over the Baroness. She stared up at me with huge, frightened eyes. As I leaned over her to unfasten a rope, I whispered, "All hell is going to break loose. When I yell, you take off—try to make it to the courtyard and wait for me. Hide if you have to. *Don't* try to help me! Got it?"

She nodded. I loosed the last of the cords binding her to the rack. I slid my hand under the edge of the rack and felt the cold butt of the Luger in its taped sling. My hand closed around it.

I shoved the girl off the rack. She went sprawling on the floor, out of the line of fire.

"NOW!"

I spun around. Wilhelmina was already at work, spitting death at the machine gunner near the door. I gave him three in the chest. The man folded and slid to the floor, the Tommy gun clattering on the stone. I shot the other man just as he was in the act of firing. The slug twitched at my jacket. The man went spinning back with a black hole between his eyes.

Events were moving with a racing fury now—like a

speeded-up film. Max Rader, his face chalky, turned and raced for the door. I plunged after him. That bar! I flicked two shots at the remaining men as I ran. They were cowering in a corner, hands over their heads. The fight was out of them.

Rader hesitated at the door, staring back in fright, then seized the heavy door and began to swing it shut. I put a bullet within an inch of his hands. I didn't want to kill Rader—I might need him for a hostage.

Rader squealed in fear and turned to run. I collided with the Baroness as we both reached the door at the same time. I snapped a shot at the retreating form of Rader, already vanishing in the gloom of the dungeon corridor. If I could get him in the leg! I missed, and heard the bullet ricochet wildly off the dripping stone walls. I swore. Rader must not get away. I scooped up my weapons concealed in the suit of armor.

I shoved the Baroness out of the way and slammed the heavy door shut just as lead began to *thunk* into it from the inside. Rader's men were getting their guts back. I dropped the bar into place. That would hold them.

I pushed the Baroness ahead of me along the passage. Rader would be getting his guts back too, any minute.

We reached a niche where a low-watt bulb gleamed yellowly. I pulled the Baroness into the recess. She strained against me, trembling, naked from the waist up. *"Mein Gott, mein Gott!"* She repeated the words over and over.

I shook her savagely. "Snap out of it, kid! No time for hysterics now! I've got to get Rader. Maybe it's already too late, but I've got to try. Here—"

I tore off my jacket and handed it to her. I put Pierre and Hugo in my trouser pockets. "Put this on. Then try to get back to the courtyard without being seen. If you can't make it, if you're cut off, then come back here!

You understand? Here. We can get out the way I came in earlier tonight."

I stepped out of the little niche and flattened myself against the wall. No shot came from the clotted shadows in the long dank corridor. I pulled the Baroness out of the niche and said, "Okay. Run for it. I'll see you when I've got Rader."

The Baroness pressed against me, her mouth seeking mine, her naked breasts warm against my chest. "Nicky— I—oh, Nicky . . ."

I pushed her away roughly. "No time for that *now*," I said savagely. "Go on, damn you!"

She ran down the dark corridor, not looking back.

I let her vanish around a corner, then I proceeded cautiously after her. My mind raced, weighing the odds, trying to establish an order of battle. Rader could make it back to the new part of the *schloss,* of course, and bar the door between the old and new sections of the castle. But would he? He would know by this time, because of the planted weapons, that I had been in the old *schloss* before and was familiar with it. That I could get in and out at will. So Rader was faced with the choice of trying to prevent our escape by covering the outside with the few men he had left, or coming in after me at once and fighting it out. And Rader had a great deal at stake. Time was against him.

I darted across a dimly lit intersection. Somewhere I could hear the faint, diminishing echo of footsteps. The Baroness, still running! The sound vanished and for a moment it was very quiet in the old dungeons. Water trickled somewhere. It was the only sound. Until—

A new sound invaded the gloom. I tensed and moved like a shadow toward another niche a few feet beyond the intersection. The sound—incredible as it was—the sound was that of a man sobbing in fear, in abject terror.

I inched along the wall toward the niche. The sobbing

continued. I was puzzled. It could be a decoy, of course, but it was a strange way to rig it. And it had to be Max Rader—who else? Maybe the vaunted courage, the badge of honor, as the man himself had called his dueling scar—maybe that was all so much hogwash. The Iron Cross meant nothing—a lot of cowardly punks had gotten that.

I moved still nearer the niche. I could smell it now, like an animal. The smell of fear. Of terror. Rader was showing his true colors now. The SS general was in a blue funk. In a moment he would be begging me not to kill him!

No, I told myself. It's too easy. Something is very wrong.

I was right back beside the niche now. The terrified sobbing continued. I shifted the Luger to my right hand and took a final look around. Only shadow. I reached into the niche and gripped a man's coat collar. I recognized the slick feel of the cloth. A dinner jacket! It *was* Rader, by God!

I yanked the sniveling man out of the recess and shoved the Luger hard into his belly. "No—no—" the man cried. "Don't kill me! For Jesus' sake don't kill me! I am not Rader—I am an old man! I do not fight you! Ahhh—don't kill me!"

"Keep still!" I snapped. "Don't move. I want a look at you." Light was beginning to dawn as I whipped the pencil flashlight from his hip pocket. Yes. I was beginning to realize how I had been duped. Played for a sucker!

I held the trembling man erect and examined him in the thin beam of light. It was Max Rader—and yet it was not. Certainly it was the man who had been behind the desk—the man in the torture chamber just now.

Now that I was close to the frightened man there was another smell. A cosmetic smell! I swiped with a finger at the dueling scar. It came off on my hand. Make-up!

Self-disgust welled in me. What a sap I had been to be

so taken in! Even though the man was a fine actor, had played his part superbly.

I dropped the man like a sack of potatoes. "Okay— whoever you are. Where's the real Rader?"

The impersonator groveled on the floor. "I don't know —I swear I don't know. Somewhere in the castle, I think. He was—he was on the gallery while we talked." The fellow began to weep openly. "Are you going to kill me? Don't—don't for God's sake. I was only doing a job. I know nothing. I did only what I was told to—"

I kicked him hard. In actuality I was kicking myself. I had been decoyed, but good! But to what purpose? What had the real Rader hoped to gain by—

A bullet splatted against the stone close to my ear. I vaulted the weeping man and slid into the niche as the report of a pistol still rang in the corridor. My question was answered. I knew where the real Rader was.

The man on the floor was still whimpering. I reached out a foot to kick him again. "Crawl back around the corner," I hissed. "Get the hell out of this, damn you."

The man obeyed, crawling out of sight like a worm. I waited in his tiny recess. In a moment Rader's voice— the real voice—came echoing down the shadowy corridor.

"Carter?" The ancient walls picked up the sound and flung it about in echo—"Carter—Carter—Carter . . ."

I didn't answer. I was busy figuring the odds again. Rader would try to stall, hold me in the recess while his men closed in. I couldn't give him any time! There was one dim light on the wall midway between them. It had to go.

"I know you're there, Carter," Rader continued. "I see you have tumbled to my little stratagem too. A pity. But it has served its purpose. Anton is really a superb actor, don't you think? But he is old and a coward, poor man. We can't really blame him. I hired him to act a part, not to fight my battles for me. I am quite capable of doing that for myself."

The voice was nearly the same, I noticed. The actor had caught most of it in his impersonation—but now something new was apparent. A hint of megalomania. Hitler had suffered from it. Delusions of grandeur. A disease that made you think you were God!

My lips thinned into a cold smile. This was the real Max Rader, all right. A rat ripe for the killing.

I felt in my pocket for my spare clip. One was all I had. Quickly I counted back—I should have one shot left in Wilhelmina, because I always carried one in the barrel.

Faster than a heartbeat I leaned out of the niche and shot out the single light in the corridor. The gloom was complete now. I leaped across to the far wall, crouching low. Rader fired too late, his pistol winking red in the blackness. Stone chips slashed at my face as the bullets keened about me. I went up the corridor toward Rader in a loose, slouching run that covered three or four yards at a bound. As I ran I slipped the new clip into the Luger.

I yelled as I ran. "Stick around, Rader! We'll shoot it out in the dark. A game of chance, Kraut! Any number can play. Anyone can win!"

Having just witnessed my shooting, Max Rader had no stomach for blind fighting. I heard him running as I reached the spot where Rader had been. The footfalls led off to the left, down another dark tunnel. I went bounding down it, silent now, gaining on the running feet ahead of him.

For an instant I wondered how the Baroness was doing. Would she make it?

Then I rounded a bend in the corridor and there was no time for wondering about anything—except how to keep alive. Max Rader had made a mistake. He had run into a dead end, an impasse!

Lead slashed around me as I ran into the room and realized what had happened. Rader had cornered himself in some sort of armory. A single barred window high on the wall let in a gust of wind and rain. One small light burned in a wire cage high on the ceiling. I dove for the protection of a heavy table as Rader's gun winked death at me from across the room. The bullet thudded into the wall beside my head.

I lay quietly behind the table and listened. I could hear Rader breathing across the room. I decided against shooting out the single light. Let Rader waste a bullet.

Rader was probably thinking the same thing, because he did not shoot at the bulb. In its fitful tawny light we both lay and listened and waited for each other to make a mistake.

I glanced around the room. An old armory. Ancient shields and weapons on the walls, all coated with rust and grime. Piles of axes and huge swords scattered all around. A rusty forge. A sagging grindstone.

The long silence was too much for Max Rader. His rat's blood began to show. He called across the room in a voice that trembled ever so slightly: "It looks like a stalemate, Carter. Care to talk it over?"

"No."

"Be reasonable, Carter. No use in shooting it out. Both of us will be killed. No one wins that way!" Rader's perfect English began to leave him under stress.

"My men will be here soon," he said. "Then you will have *no* chance! Better we talk, *nein?*"

I laughed coldly. *"Nein!* They won't be here. You know it. They're worrying about their own skins now. How much do you want to bet that they're running like hell?"

Rader broke into a torrent of German curses. Suddenly, he lost his nerve completely and broke for the door, firing at me as he came. A slug went through my shirt without wounding me. Another branded me lightly on the right thigh.

I shot him four times in the chest at close range.

I stood over the dying man, watching his eyes glaze. I kicked Rader's gun away from the limp hand. I bent and grabbed a handful of the man's hair and lifted his head, studying the dead face carefully. The man *had* had a face job! I could see the new pink scars around the ears and eyes and under the chin. He looked very like the actor —or vice versa—except for a nasty vulturine quality that no surgeon's knife could hide.

I ran my fingers over the dead face and felt the dueling scar. This one was real enough. There was a lump beneath the skin. I smiled. It figured. I took Hugo from my pocket and slashed at the dead face. I fumbled in the wound and brought out a shiny length of metal, matching the fragment of key I had taken from Hondo's false teeth. So there it was. Two halves make a whole. All I had to do now was walk into the bank and claim the golden tiger. I grinned. It wasn't quite that simple. Not yet.

I straightened as I heard the soft slip of shoe leather on stone. I recognized the step. The Baroness.

I glanced swiftly around. I found a rusty old mace, a fearful weapon studded with nasty spikes. I swung it three or four times, then tossed it away. I was standing looking down at the smashed face of Rader when the Baroness entered the room. She had her little pistol in her hand.

"Don't look at him," I warned her. "I had to shoot him in the face. It'll give you nightmares."

She ignored the warning. She pushed past him and stood gazing for a moment at the battered features. "At last," she said softly. "At last the pig is dead. And so crushed—" She smiled grimly at me. "As I said before— his own mother would not know him."

"Right," I said. I watched a little pistol in her hand. The Baroness turned away from the body. With her back to me she pulled up one leg of her slacks and tucked the gun away.

"What are you doing back here?" I asked. "Couldn't you make it out?"

"No. They've barred the door leading into the new part. I had to come back. I waited where you told me to, Nicky, but when you didn't come, I got scared. I came to find you." She flung herself into my arms, pressing her lithe body against mine. "Oh, God, Nicky—get me out of here! I can't stand any more!"

I held her gently. I fastened my jacket around her more securely, concealing the thrusting white breasts.

"I will," I promised. "You'll get a little wet, but you'll get out. We'll go the way I came in—the way Hondo found. I'll call and have an AXE man pick us up and take us to the hotel. The Swiss police can worry about all this mess."

Her lips roved over my face. "And you'll stay with me? At least for a time? I—I don't want to be alone just now, Nicky. I—I want you to hold me and make love to me. Forever and ever!"

"Forever is a long time," I said. "So we'd better get started."

Sixteen

The storm still raged outside the baroque windows of the Excelsior Hotel. Inside, in my room, another storm was just reaching a climax. The Baroness screamed and clawed at me, her lovely body arched in frenzy. I myself was high on an exploding cloud.

Then it was over and I was acutely conscious of the dawn outside and of a growing coldness within the room. Within myself. Now it had to be faced.

I left her breathing softly, half asleep, and went to the bathroom. When I came out I turned on the bright ceiling light and began to dress. I watched her in the dresser mirror. Saw her open her lavender-gray eyes and stare at me in puzzlement.

I had retrieved Gladstone from the hotel checkroom and was enjoying the luxury of a clean shirt and tie. As I knotted the latter, the Baroness spoke: "Nicky, darling! What are you doing? Surely you're not going so soon!"

"Surely I am," I said. I shrugged into my jacket. I checked Wilhelmina, Pierre, and Hugo. All in their proper places.

I faced the bed. "I'm on my way," I told her. "And I would advise you to do the same, honey. I'm going to give you a break—not that you deserve it, but it goes against my grain to turn in a woman I've made love to. Such beautiful love, too," I added cynically. "You're quite an expert, baby. But then, you're an expert in a lot of things. Mainly in telling lies."

174

The Baroness sat bolt upright in the bed, her face quivering with shock and hurt. She did not bother to cover her breasts.

"What on earth are you talking about? Have you gone mad?"

"I'm mad, all right," I said grimly. "Mad at myself. You nearly took me, baby! You really did! I damned near fell for it—and for you. But you can cut out the play-acting now—the game's over."

She held out her arms to me, her lovely features twisted in anguish. "Nicky, my darling! Please don't talk like that. Come—come to me. Hold me. Tell me what is wrong."

For an insane moment I felt a desire to go to her, to hold her and kiss her, take her again. She had the power, this bitch. And knew how to use it. At the moment she looked like all the lovely strumpets in the world, sitting there with her arms outstretched and her breasts ready for kisses. Then the moment passed and I was once again KILLMASTER.

"You've been working with Max Rader from the beginning," I told her. "Probably for years. I wouldn't know about that. Somehow you wormed yourself into West German intelligence. You pretended to hate Rader. You even wore that locket to help the lie along."

She opened her mouth to protest, but I held up my hand to silence her. "Let me finish. Then you can tell me where I'm wrong, if it matters. You and Max were old buddies. I can't quite figure how or why, but you must have been. You kept him posted on everything that went on. That's how he knew things were hotting up again. That he was going to be tried again. And how he knew an AXE agent was being sent to Geneva to intercept him when he tried for the tiger. You knew he had had his face changed, sure, but you didn't mention it to your people until you, or Max, saw how you could use it to your own advantage."

I was pacing the room now, keeping my eye on the woman in the bed. "Either you or Max hit on the idea of using someone to impersonate him. That actor, whatever his name was, was to be pointed out to me as the *real* Max Rader. You were going to finger *him!* While Max and Hondo, with me off on a wild-goose chase, sneaked into the bank and out again with the tiger. That actor was good, I'll say that. Really terrific. What *was* his name?"

"Chak. Anton Chak. He's an old has-been. He's been nearly starving for ten years." It was no slip of the tongue. She had given up. Her face was sullen as she regarded me. She reached for the sheet and covered her naked breasts. I smiled faintly at the gesture. Lovers no more!

I nodded at her. "Good kid. I'm glad to see you're through playing games. You want to tell me about it now?"

The Baroness bit her lip. "What are you going to do with me?"

I shrugged. "Me? Nothing. I told you—I'll give you a head start, baby. I don't know where in hell you can run to, but you can try."

Tears welled in her eyes. "Oh, Nicky! I—I wish it could be different. Everything I did and said was not a lie! Really not. I—I could love you, Nicky!"

"In my profession," I said, "that word is nonexistent." I glanced at my watch. "Get on with it. I've got work to do."

The Baroness took a cigarette from the bedside table and lit it. She stared at me through the gray smoke, her red lips pouting. "Yes," she said finally. "I am a liar. I have had to be. To survive. We lost the war, remember. Through no fault of our own. We were betrayed—betrayed by fools and cowards like my father!"

I whistled softly. "So that's it. *Heil Hitler!*"

She stiffened. Her eyes burned at me. "Yes! *Heil Hitler!* I was of the Hitler Youth. I hated my father—he was against everything I stood for. I was glad when they hanged him. I made Max take me to see it. He did not want to, but I insisted. I loved every minute of it—my father deserved to be hanged. He had betrayed the Reich! He tried to kill our great leader!"

Pity and anger mingled in me. In a way it really wasn't her fault. Hitler had said "Give me the children!" They had done a good job on this one.

My stomach churned as a thought struck me. I went to the foot of the bed and stared at her. The Baroness glared back defiantly.

I said: "You turned your father in, didn't you? You found out about the plot somehow—a kid could do that —and then you informed on your own father!"

"He was a traitor!"

I had my answer. I felt sick for a moment, then brushed it off. It happened. It happened all the time. I was in a filthy business—no need to complain if it made me want to spew now and then.

I began to pace again. "Then what? After they hanged your father, did they give you a medal?"

"No. I got no attention at all. I was secret, to be hidden, to wait for the future."

They never gave up.

"I became Max Rader's mistress," the Baroness said. "I did not love him—I never did. I could never stand him, physically. But it was my duty! He was a soldier of the Reich."

"A bit young for that, weren't you?"

"I was old enough. And" —here the Baroness allowed a ghost of a smile to touch her lips— "I—I had other interests. I had my lovers."

"I'll bet. Like the Comtesse?"

The lovely sleek shoulders moved in a shrug. "Among others. I am not really like that, as I told you. The Comtesse had money. And she is not in this thing, in case you were wondering. She knows nothing."

Hawk would have checked that out by now. I nodded. "Okay. So Rader was running and you saw your chance to decoy me away from him. But you fouled it up on the steamer coming over from Thonon. You couldn't be sure I was an AXE man, but Rader's men followed us to the Hotel Lux just in case. When you *were* sure about me, it was too late—Hondo had messed things up by butting in and losing his teeth. And I had his half of the key. That must have had you pretty confused, huh?"

The Baroness seemed more at ease now. She smiled at me through the smoke of her cigarette. "That had nothing to do with me. My job was to point out the wrong man to you—to identify Anton Chak as Rader and send you chasing after him. Max had told me about the French key, of course, but I was to have no part in that. I did nothing, you saw. I did not try to get it, or find where you hid it. I left that up to Max. Anyway, I could not communicate with him—I thought it best to stick tightly to you, my Nicky!" The Baroness smiled at him. "I am glad I did. You *are* a splendid man, Nicky!"

She sighed as she stubbed out her cigarette. "I wouldn't have minded staying at the villa with you for weeks, darling."

"But you didn't know about Osman, did you? That he was working for Rader too?"

She frowned. "No. I do not understand that part. Osman, of all people. Max knew of my friendship with the Comtesse, of course. He knew I visited the villa often. But—"

"Simple," I said. "*Rader* didn't even trust you. He hired Osman just to keep an eye on you, long before this tiger thing broke. In a way you're pretty lucky, Baroness. If Rader had succeeded in getting the tiger, with your help, I don't think he would have been grateful. I think you might have joined our friend Hondo."

I thought she shuddered a little. She crossed her arms over her breasts as if she were cold. "I will admit, my

Nicky, that the same thought had crossed my mind. I came not to trust Max—I do not think he was worrying about the Reich at the last. He was greedy for himself only."

"Yet you played along with him. You went to him as soon as I gave you a chance—yesterday in the Civil Gardens. You pretended that this Anton Chak was Rader—you pretended to be in mortal danger. You were almost crazy with fear! That was a good act you put on, incidentally. That bit on the rack in the torture chamber. You damn near had me sold then. I was even feeling sorry for you, but I had to do it. I had to get Rader and his men into that chamber, where I had planted my weapons."

She was gazing at me with an odd light in her gray eyes. "And when did you become unsold, my Nicky?"

I laughed harshly. "When I found the actor whimpering like a baby. I never really did trust you, but that clinched it. You had let me think Chak was Rader. You were damned then and you knew it. That was why you came snooping after me, pistol in hand. You wanted to find out if I knew the truth. If I had killed the actor thinking he was Rader. If I had, and I did know the truth, then you were going to kill me. But I fooled you, baby. I smashed Rader's face up so you couldn't recognize him—you didn't know at first whether I had killed Chak or Rader! And if I had really shot him in the face, as I told you, I wouldn't have known either! So maybe your little game wasn't blown yet. You thought! So you played along and here you are."

I picked up the rhino-hide suitcase and went to the door. I said, "I'm turning you in, of course. Better run for it, honey, while you have time. I almost hope you get away. You're too beautiful to spend the rest of your life in prison."

"Nicky." Her voice was low, soft, sweet.

I turned at the door. She was smiling from the bed, her little pistol in her hand.

"Sit down, Nicky. Please. Don't make me kill you, *liebling*. But I cannot let you go now. Unless we can make a bargain."

I scowled. "No bargains."

She pouted her red mouth at me. "Then I shall have to kill you, my Nicky. My little gun makes not much noise. But it kills very well. I know. I am very sorry, darling, but I cannot let you tell the truth about me. I will not get any of the treasure, that is true, but I can arrange a story about your death and go back to my work."

"You're being a fool," I said roughly. "And you are wearing my patience thin."

She pointed the gun directly at my chest. Her finger tightened on the trigger. "I have said I am sorry, Nicky. I am. I could almost have loved you!"

She pulled the trigger. I laughed.

"No good, Baroness. I pulled your little teeth the first night at the villa. I took the powder out of the shells."

Her face twisted in disbelief and rage. She pointed the gun at me again and pulled the trigger over and over. Nothing but a series of flat clicks.

"Gott verdampt!" She hurled the little pistol at me. I fended it off with an elbow. She stared at me with a face gone suddenly haggard. Beauty and coquetry fled before stark reality. The Baroness made a stifled sound in her throat and buried her face in the pillow.

I took something from my pocket and tossed it to her. "There," I said softly. "One bullet. I saved it just for you."

I left her.

—

Seventeen

The little tiger glinted dully in the light from Hawk's desk lamp. The ruby eyes, sparking and refracting the light, reminded me of blood. This was natural, I supposed. A lot of blood had been shed over this golden image. Probably more would be shed in the future. That, however, was not my concern at the moment.

Hawk spoke around his cigar, unlit as usual. "Take a good look at it, son. It'll be your last. It leaves for Indonesia tonight under special guard."

I reached to stroke the gleaming golden hide. I picked it up and inspected the underbelly—I could barely make out the thin seam running from chest to tail, the only sign that the tiger had been gutted and then carefully restored.

I put the tiger down. "So it was what was *in* the tiger that you really wanted? Your men did a good job—you can hardly tell it was opened."

Hawk nodded. "What State wanted, you mean. I was only obeying orders, just like you. But this was a hot one, N3. As hot as they come. Not even Ivan knew about it. Thank God! If the Russians had been in on this there would have been all hell to pay. And if *they* had gotten the tiger the West would be in even more trouble than we're in now."

I got up and began to pace Hawk's office. It was over now, the tension gone. I was always restless after a job.

Hawk had flown to Geneva yesterday. He and I and a

181

representative of the West German Government had opened Goering's vault in the bank of Paul Chardet et Fils. Through a slight oversight, Hawk explained with a straight face, the Indonesian representative had been overlooked. Bad protocol, of course, and a regrettable lapse. But those things happened.

An hour later Hawk and I were on the way back to Washington. We traveled by military plane with a special Marine guard. The crate in which the golden tiger traveled was never out of our sight.

West Germany was claiming the balance of the loot found in Hermann Goering's vault. Most of it, Hawk said, would probably go to pay off war claims and for reparations. Fitting that it should.

The Swiss police, tipped off by an anonymous phone call, had found nothing in the Schloss Brunhild but dead bodies. The same with the Villa Limbo. If one believed the radio and the Swiss papers the police were in a high state of indignation. Someone had again been playing international games on Swiss territory and leaving a mess behind.

Now Hawk said: "You did a fine job, Nick. Take a week off and try to stay out of trouble."

"Thanks. It will be a pleasure." I started for the door, then halted. "I'm a little curious, damn it, though I know it's against the rules. I don't suppose you would care to give me a hint as to what *was* in the tiger?"

Hawk came near to smiling. He tossed away his old cigar and jabbed a new one in his lean old face. He did not light it. "I might," he said. "Just a hint. Off the record and never to be mentioned?"

"Of course."

"Okay. It was a master plan for what you might call Operation Fourth Reich. Fat Hermann was the cleverest of the lot. He knew the war was lost long before the others did. So he started planning for the future. He didn't plan on being hanged."

"He wasn't."

Hawk nodded. "I know. I said he was the smartest. He had the tiger hollowed out and hid the master papers in it. Cadre lists of the youngsters, German kids, who were even then being smuggled abroad. Who were to grow up as citizens of other countries, all innocent and above-board—until *Der Tag!*"

The Day! I remembered the look on the Baroness' face. No—they never gave up.

"But preparations had to be made for these new Nazis," Hawk said. "They would need arms, materiel—everything. But mostly they would need money. That's where the twenty submarines come in.

"After the war," Hawk went on, "the Germans came up twenty subs short. Not on the surface, of course. They squared on the records. But when the CIA finally got around to it they found that the Germans built twenty subs that were never accounted for. One of the builders talked eventually. But no one knew what had become of the subs."

Hawk pointed to the gleaming tiger. "There was a chart in his belly, along with other records. There were twenty crosses, with careful fixes and soundings for each. They scattered them all over the world—near each pole, off the African coast, the Korea Straits, Yellow Sea—even one in Puget Sound. All in relatively shallow water. Waiting."

I whistled. "The cagey bastards! They know how to plan. You've got to give them that."

Hawk regarded the chewed end of the cigar. "They do. But so do we. And we hit the jackpot, thanks to you. We'll raise all those subs and use the loot to try and promote peace instead of war. And we've got the cadre lists, too. Those German kids who were exported twenty years ago will be watched. We'll give them a chance to forget it and go straight—but they'll be watched."

I started for the door again. "Thanks for telling me about it, sir. I'll take that week off, I think."

"Nick!"

I halted at the door and turned. "Sir?"

Hawk took a flimsy from a wire basket on his desk and held it out. "This might interest you. It clears up another loose end."

Nick glanced at the flimsy. It was brief and to the point. The Baroness Elizabeth von Stadt had been found dead in a hotel room in Paris. A single bullet from a small-caliber pistol had been fired into her brain. The Paris police were calling it suicide.

I gave the chief a questioning look. "Suicide? You think so, sir? She made the West Germans look pretty bad. They must be having a real house cleaning."

Hawk squinted his eyes at me. "Your guess is as good as mine. She made us look pretty bad too, but we didn't kill her. Anyway, it isn't as bad as it seemed at first— she was only working with Rader. No one else. The few bits and pieces she could have picked up wouldn't amount to much in the big picture. Only where the tiger was concerned. And neither she nor Rader knew what was *in* the tiger."

I nodded slowly. I wondered if the Baroness had gone to her old friend the Comtesse for help—and had not found it. She might, then, with the West Germans hard after her, have turned to her legacy from me. The bullet.

I said good-bye to Hawk and went out into a crisp September day. There was a lot of pedestrian traffic on DuPont Circle, most of it made up of pretty girls with marvelous legs. I heartily approved. I lit a cigarette and stood for a few minutes watching the show. More than one girl smiled tentatively at me.

I walked away. Somewhere there was a bottle of wine and a girl waiting for me. It was the way you started forgetting the old and looking forward to the new.

It shouldn't take long to find them.

AWARD

NICK CARTER

Don't Miss a Single
Killmaster Spy Chiller·

SAIGON   Nick Carter
A cauldron where each caress can lead to sudden mayhem.   AX0625—60¢

AMSTERDAM   Nick Carter
A wanton blonde is the only lead to a private spy network.   AX0628—60¢

TEMPLE OF FEAR   Nick Carter
N3 assumes the identity of a man long dead.
     AX0629—60¢

MISSION TO VENICE   Nick Carter
A missing H-bomb triggers a game of global blackmail.
     AX0632—60¢

A KOREAN TIGER   Nick Carter
N3 must recover stolen nuclear plans that can crush America to dust.   AX0634—60¢

THE MIND POISONERS   Nick Carter
A vicious international plot hooks American college kids on a violence drug.   AX0636—60¢

THE CHINA DOLL   Nick Carter
Nick Carter is the first white man in the "Forbidden City" of Peking.   AX0638—60¢

CHECKMATE IN RIO   Nick Carter
Sex and savagery are the facts of life for every agent.
     AX0639—60¢

Hard-Hitting Novels Based on Today's Top Motion Pictures

PLAY MISTY FOR ME   Paul J. Gillette
A major motion picture starring Clint Eastwood—now a compelling novel of violence that will tie you in knots! AS0907—75¢

DUCK YOU SUCKER!   James Lewis
A fortune in gold and two men with an impossible plan to rob it! A wild Western—now a great motion picture starring Rod Steiger and James Coburn.   AS0831—75¢

BORN TO WIN   Mike Roote
A tough, taut, terrible, and tender portrait of a junkie and his world. A smash new motion picture starring George Segal, Paula Prentiss, Karen Black.   AS0899—75¢

SABATA   Brian Fox
It didn't take long for the town to learn that Sabata was a man of few words, many talents—and a deadeye draw. A blazing western novel!   AS0741—75¢

SEE NO EVIL   William Hughes
You won't know what terror is until you read this spellbinding novel of murder and violence. A movie suspense thriller!
AS0895—75¢

THE McMASTERS   Dean Owen
A white man, a black man, a beautiful Indian woman—they didn't stand a chance in a hate-filled town ... *and they didn't give a damn!*   AS0544—75¢

THE CAT O'NINE TAILS   Paul J. Gillette
A blind man, a little girl, and a reporter all try to escape from a ruthless killer in this novel of the movie suspense thriller!
AS0870—75¢

Action-Packed Westerns

THE GOOD, THE BAD, THE UGLY Joe Millard
They formed an alliance of hate to steal a fortune in dead man's gold! A blazing new Western! AX0918—60¢

A COFFIN FULL OF DOLLARS Joe Millard
The Man With No Name, Shadrach, Apachito—a legendary threesome out for each other's blood with a coffin full of dollars the winner's take-home pay! AX0856—60¢

FOR A FEW DOLLARS MORE Joe Millard
The trigger-tempered loner from the Award "Dollar" Western series matches wits and bullets with the most desperate gang in the West! AX0919—60¢

A DOLLAR TO DIE FOR Brian Fox
No men ever killed in colder blood than the desperate foursome led by the gun-ready hero, The Man With No Name! AX0917—60¢

DEAD RINGER Brian Fox
Two fast-talking, sharp-shooting mavericks—more brash and wild than Butch Cassidy and The Sundance Kid! Based on the ABC-TV series "Alias Smith & Jones." AS0896—75¢

LAWMAN Grant Freeling
He lived his own brand of justice—and his star was a license to kill! Now a major motion picture starring Burt Lancaster, Robert Ryan, Lee J. Cobb. AS0851—75¢

THE GUNFIGHTER Martin Ryerson
Morgan Royal, a two-fisted lawman—the man who had hunted down Quantrill after the Civil War—challenges a gang of killers ... and is trapped in a powdersmoke hell! AX0653—60¢

SECRET MISSION

*"...the best new
adventure and intrigue series
to come along in years"*
(Archer Winston, The New York *Post*)

SECRET MISSION: PEKING   Don Smith
A faulty black-market computer, sold to the Red Chinese, may
trigger World War III!   AX0297—60¢

SECRET MISSION: PRAGUE   Don Smith
Five-million dollars worth of guns are set to level an entire coun-
try. Phil Sherman must face death many times to stop them.
AX0353—60¢

SECRET MISSION: CORSICA   Don Smith
A million Americans are doomed to die unless Phil Sherman
can untangle the secret of a Chinese-controlled narcotics jungle.
AX0358—60¢

SECRET MISSION: MOROCCO   Don Smith
A bizarre duplicate of James Bond's Goldfinger—one who has
already robbed Fort Knox!—is behind a world-wide plan to
murder U. S. agents.   AX0393—60¢

SECRET MISSION: ISTANBUL   Don Smith
A Soviet master spy will defect to the U. S.—if Phil Sherman can
kidnap his young nymphomaniac wife from a Red security prison.
AX0446—60¢

SECRET MISSION: TIBET   Don Smith
Sherman must destroy a Chinese death ray wrecking U. S. and
Russian space ships. His only ally—the American traitor who
built the weapon for Red China!   AX0522—60¢

SECRET MISSION: CAIRO   Don Smith
A stolen atomic bomb hair-triggered to explode on touch buried
somewhere in Egypt. Agent Sherman must find and disarm it—
at any cost, *even his own life!*   AX0591—60¢